"Whether therefore you
eat or drink,
or whatsoever you do,
do all to the glory of
God."
1Cor. 10:31.

...'So you're saying you couldn't do such a thing to any of your female staff?"

'You know I wouldn't. That's not my style. If there's any lady I'm interested in, I'll come out neat and clear. It's no fun if a man has to use force or threats. But besides, I am a Christian, that makes a major difference."

There seemed to be some powerful current flowing between them now...

...There was some minutes silence, as Ben thought of the next question to ask her. "Is there any man in your life?"

Tolu's eyes popped open. "That's too direct."

Ben laughed. "It was intended to be. So?"

Tolu heaved a sigh. "None yet, I'm still praying," Her heart was pounding now.

"Let me give you one more prayer point. Pray about me."...

...She wasn't sure of what to say, so she uttered the first thing that came to her mind. "What about your girl?" She tried to sound casual...

In Love FOR US

Taiwo Iredele Odubiyi

REDELS TECHNIQUES LTD.
10, Salako Street, Mushin - Lagos, Nigeria.
℡01-7738610, 08033043443

Dedication

This book is dedicated to
The Lord Jesus Christ
and to
my Pastors and beloved parents in
Christ, Pastors Taiwo and Bimbo
Odukoya, whose ministries made me
to *discover* myself, hence these series
of novels.

" Without a doubt, your love for God
and His word, your passion for souls,
your faithfuness and integrity in
ministry has made me what I am
today."

IN LOVE FOR US

Printed in Nigeria.
ISBN 978-34540-4-8

For information:
REDELS TECHNIQUES LTD.
10, Salako Street, Mushin, Lagos-Nigeria.
Tel: (01) 7738610, 08033043443.

Acknowledgement

To God be the glory, "Who worketh in us both to will and to do of His good pleasure."

To my husband and my Pastor, Sola, who has been consistent in loving me consistently for over twelve years. *You deserve a medal!*

To Tioluwani, Tanitoluwawa, Tirenioluwa. *Thanks for understanding that Mummy had to write. You are God's gifts to me.*

To the Soyombos and the Odubiyis, *I just want to say again - I love you and thanks.*

To Bode, Yomi, Chime, Bro. Fash, Ebun, Rev. Sokoya, and of course, Bro. Biodun Balogun, *Thank you.*

To Dr. Akindele, Gbenga Oluyemi, Kemi Sobayo and Barr. Opeyemi Okusanya, thanks for going through the scripts.

To FOUNTAINEERS Ikorodu *What do you see? Spread your wings and soar!!*

To the **SINGLESLINK** family. *This is what you have been waiting for, there is more to come, I love you!!!*

Pastor (Mrs.) Taiwo Iredele Odubiyi

Ikorodu - Lagos, Nigeria.

CHAPTER
ONE

Ben sat down on his chair heavily. He had just returned from a meeting with the commissioner and he intended to relax a little, probably have a cold drink, before going to see the Managing Director of Liteace Merchant Bank. The Bank was one of the many customers of Wright Ally Computers Company, owned by Ben. The Bank had just paid for the com puters it bought from Wright Ally, but needed to purchase more, worth eight million naira. Ben decided to see the Managing Director himself to agree the terms of payment with him.

He looked round his office, and smiled a little to himself, pleased with what he saw. It had the look of wealth. The wall of the room was cream, and a company particularly known to be an expert at such handled the interior decoration. Who could have thought he would own such a big company today? Six years ago, nobody knew him. He was a struggling young man. Those were tough, cruel days.

The secretary came in and dropped a white envelope on the table, just in front of him.

"This is for you sir."

"Thank you Kemi," He started, picking up the envelope. "could you give me a bottle of malt and probably ..." He stopped abruptly. He had turned the envelope over and saw the name written at the back - FROM TOLU! The name leapt at him. Could it be Tolu - one of the workers in "*Love of God Assembly*" the church he attended?

But it wasn't likely. They just knew each other to be members of the same church. There would not be any reason for her to come to his office. There was only one other Tolu - could it be her?

With impatience, he tore the envelope open, reading the letter that was inside with narrow–eyed intensity. It was from the other Tolu, his ex- girlfriend, whom he hadn't seen for the past six years since she changed her mind about their relationship, or should he say since her parents changed her mind? But it couldn't be! What would she want?

He looked at his watch. It was 3.15 pm. She would come back at 4 pm according to the letter and she would be needing his assistance.

"You were saying that I should bring a bottle of malt and something sir." The dark complexioned secretary said, her voice slicing through his thoughts.

He had forgotten she was still around. "Just malt," he said flatly. The secretary went out with a little smile on her face, wondering whom the letter was from and its content.

TOLU PRATT! His heart started to beat wildly. How did she know where to find him? Would she have changed? She was 5 feet 7 inches tall, fair skinned. That meant she didn't travel abroad, she was still in town. But Lagos must be big, because they never once met in the past six years. Ben ran a hand through his hair with annoyance- *but why am I disturbed like this?* Sadness swept over him as he thought of her, her love and tenderness.

They had been going out together for almost two years when eventually her parents forced her to leave him. Not that they ever approved of the relationship, he thought angrily. They thought Ben was not good enough for their beautiful daughter. Yes, Tolu was beautiful. With her fair, flawless, glowing skin, long hair and a set of white teeth which she readily revealed in a smile, she was the epitome of beauty. And the fact that he was from Ogun State didn't help matters.

The secretary came in, carrying a tray, on which was a bottle of malt and a glass cup.

"At what time did the lady come?" Ben enquired with the letter still in his hand.

"Em - around 2pm sir," Kemi responded, noticing the little frown on her boss' face. This was her second year with Wright Ally Computers Company, a major computer sales and Service Company. She enjoyed working for Ben. He was an excellent employer who knew how to be firm and strict when he had to be, and could also be scrupulously fair and ready to listen to his staff. She had planned to ask him to give her a day off during the week, so she could take her son to the clinic, but she didn't think now was a good time to ask him for favour and definitely not something like a day off. She took a look at Ben again. He looked handsome. Little wonder some girls in the office were having romantic thoughts of fantasy, trying to work their way into his heart, the secretary thought wryly. But thank God he was a believer. He had a wonderful way of handling such girls without causing any hurt feelings. He was sensible enough not to be susceptible to that kind of flattery or temptation.

She looked at Ben with admiration. *I will ask him for the day off tomorrow, when he is in a better mood,* Kemi told herself as she poured the malt into the glass cup.

Lifting it to his mouth, Ben asked coolly, "How is your family Kemi?"

"Fine sir." *But I need Thursday off,* she almost added, but she bit it back. This wasn't the right moment.

Ben turned to the computer monitor on his table. "Right, fill me in on the progress of Tuteale Company and let me have the letters from them." He ordered briskly. The secretary went into detail, discussing the matter under consideration.

She went briefly to her office, and came back with a file, spreading the sheets in it on the table for Ben's perusal.

Ben forgot completely the passage of time and, momentarily, Tolu.

A little movement in the secretary's office made the two of them to look up from the papers they had been studying. The secretary dashed quickly to her office to see who had come.

Ben heard voices, and he glanced at his watch - it was 3.55pm. Could it be Tolu? "The lady is around sir." The secretary interrupted his thoughts.

"Show her in." He said blandly.

Tolu squared her shoulders before she lost courage and tapped lightly on the door. Nervously, she pushed open the door and walked in. As she came in, she was aware of his eyes on her as they silently surveyed her, taking in the yellow gown she was wearing. This disturbed her and made her feel self conscious. Flustered, Tolu looked at Ben and saw the face that had haunted her memories for years. *How time flies*. He had not changed much although he had filled out a little, and had grown older as she heard. But he was no less handsome. He wore a well tailored dark suit with a white shirt and a silk tie, all of quality, Tolu recognized. He looked very attractive and comfortable. *How old now? Thirty years?*

"So I was not mistaken, it is you."

"Good evening, Ben." She said, forcing a smile. Was he glad to see her or irritated? She tried to read his facial expression, to know what he felt, but saw nothing.

Ben got up to shake her hand, "Good evening. Tolu. How are you?" He said with a half smile. Not even his voice had changed. It was still deep and confident.

"Fine thank you. And you?"

"Fine. Please sit down."

As they shook hands, Tolu caught the familiar scent of him, bringing the half forgotten past into her mind. She sat down nervously. There were a million butterflies in her stomach.

"You were the last person I expected to see today."

Tolu smiled shyly, "Yes, I know." She wanted Ben to say something to put her at ease, at least for old times sake - or would that be asking for too much?

She felt Ben's gaze on her face, still appraising her, but it revealed nothing of what he was thinking. His feelings were well masked. This might prove to be much harder than she had imagined, She shivered a little, feeling a tremor of alarm.

"I was here earlier on, and left a note for you," she

fumbled for words.

Please God, take control - she muttered under her breath. *Ben say something*, she prayed.

"Yep." His response was flat. It appeared he was not going to cooperate. But what did she expect, the red carpet, after the way she treated him? Not likely, Tolu reasoned. But it was not really her fault, was it? She was confused and under pressure from her parents. Then young and immature, she did not know a lot of things.

"How are your parents?" Tolu found her voice again.

"They are fine." Neither his answer nor his attitude was very forthcoming, Tolu acknowledged. "So to what do I owe the pleasure of this visit?" Ben asked, obviously not ready for small talk.

She might as well go straight to the point. She had stupidly believed that while situations changed, people stayed the same, but this wasn't so. "I'm sorry to disturb you, but I actually need your ...er, er... help, I mean ...er... your assistance." She paused.

"Well?" Ben prompted in a business like tone. She was nervous, he could see that, from the way she bit her lower lip and clenched her fists, and the wide dilated pupils of her eyes also showed her uneasiness.

"I ran into Yvonne last week and happened to mention to her that em - about my un-employment and she gave me your address that you may be able to help."

It was finally said, they were definitely the hardest words she had ever had to utter, and they were greeted by silence. *Well, let him think what he liked.* She had prayed concerning this job issue and she was sure God could turn the king's heart anyway He wanted, and could also make her enemies become her friends - including Ben. He was not acting friendly at all.

A lot of thoughts ran through Ben's mind as he stared at her. He could very well do without this trouble. He had closed that chapter of his life, or so he thought. He had imagined he was safe and secure from all alarms that could come from Tolu's end in his life, he no longer cared for her, but now it appeared he was wrong.

"You're looking for a job?" Ben queried with a frown. *God, how can I have her working with me?* He felt threatened. *It's not possible* - he reasoned.

Tolu gave him a straight look. "Yes, and I would actually appreciate whatever help you can render. I was working with Amman and Roche, but had to resign last year for some reasons, and - em - since then I've been trying to secure another one. Yvonne told me you own this place. It looks like you've done well for yourself." Tolu told him appreciatively.

No thanks to you - Ben said within himself, but to her he said, "Thank God." He thought for a while, "You have qualified as an Accountant?" His voice was low. Her perfume teased him with a soft fragrance.

"Yes." Tolu answered, drawing a steadying breath. She looked at the room, her gaze taking in its luxurious furnishing, a Television set complete with video compact disc player was on top of a table to her right.

As she took stock of the office, Ben took stock of her. She must be twenty seven years now, as he remembered he was three years older than she was. As he appraised her, he could smell the perfume she was wearing. She appeared to have lost a little weight but none the less still very beautiful, he noticed. Tolu wore a yellow silk dress that had a black collar with black buttons down the front, and she had on big yellow earrings. With her flawless skin and long hair, she looked very elegant, which gave her the image of confidence and sophistication, although what she felt inside was far from confidence. Her hair had always been long. It was one of the things he had loved about her.

She would probably be married now. Ben looked at her hand to see if she had a wedding ring on, but he could not see because of the table that separated them.

Well, what did it matter? he dismissed the thought. There was no chance of their coming together again anyway after all, he was now a Christian, *and the Bible says in 2 Corinthians 6:14, that one should not be unequally yoked together with an unbeliever, for what fellowship has righteousness with unrighteousness?*

He took up his pen idly, and tapped it on the table before he said, "Do you have your C.V. here?"

Tolu opened the black leather bag that was on her laps, and brought out the C.V. As she handed it over to him, she noticed he had no wedding ring on.

Tolu marvelled that they were behaving like two strangers. No one could have guessed they had a relationship and used to be so much in love sometime ago. In fact, there was a time she thought she was pregnant for him. Remembering made her feel like laughing, but at that time when it happened, it was not a laughing matter at all - far from it. In fact she had almost cried her eyes out.

She was twenty years old at that time while Ben was twenty three. She could still remember vividly his reaction to the news of her pregnancy. "But I thought we were careful. It is not possible!" He had said, as if he was expecting her to say she was just pulling his legs. He looked worried.

She too was perplexed. How was she going to tell her parents? What would they say? And most importantly, what would they do? They would probably kill her.

She was in her second year in the University, studying Accountancy. She had dreamt of graduating and becoming some important personality in the society, but that would never be again - she had thought at that time. Instead, there would be a baby, or with her kind of luck, there might be more than one baby, there would be diapers, feeding bottles and there would be 2 am feeding. She was so sad she could commit suicide.

"I don't know how it happened. I am five days late already," she had replied, wailing. Ben too felt his world was crashing around him, coming to a miserable end, but he could not bear how she was crying, after all, he was involved too.

He felt responsible, and for the moment, he knew he had to be a man, so Ben had pulled her to himself, used his handkerchief to clean her face.

"We'll think of something, but I want you to know I'm with you in this, all the way," he said, trying to sound calm. He had graduated just a year before and he had his own plans, which did not include a baby until much later. His father was right after all, he thought, using his right hand to rub Tolu's back, who was still sobbing, but quietly.

He remembered his father had told him if he was not ready for a baby, he should not play games that could produce one. Should he suggest abortion to her? With the kind of girl she was, she would probably never agree to it. Anyway, he remembered a friend told him how a certain girl had died last month through abortion.

But it had turned out to be a false alarm, when two days after the wailing, sobbing and sniffing, she found out she wasn't pregnant after all. Was she glad? That was seven years ago.

Tolu regarded Ben steadily, who was still looking at the C. V. in his hand, and she was glad to be able to look at him unnoticed.

Ben's gaze went to marital status and saw "single" written there. He was surprised but somehow he felt some relief.

He breathed deeply. "Well, let me keep this. I'll see what I can do. I'm not promising anything though." He said, clearly non-committal, not able to prevent the feelings of irritation and disturbance that were colouring his mood.

Her heart sank. "When would you like me to check back?" She paused and with a smile she continued, "Although it's funny, but I thought you would want to help me." There was a note of desperation in her voice.

She had always been straight forward and frank, Ben remembered, and he used to admire it, but now he felt a tinge of annoyance and resentment. "I haven't said I won't help, but it's not exactly as easy as you think. And then I'm seeing you for the first time in six years, there are things to be considered. Were you really expecting I would ask you to start right away? In case you didn't know, I had planned on spending the rest of my life without seeing you again." Ben said, sounding a little harsh, his expression hardening. He didn't intend to sound as mean as he did, but he was torn in two ways. On one hand, he felt like seizing the opportunity of employing her immediately so as to have her back around him. On the other hand, he felt why should he employ her. How could she come here and expect him to employ her immediately?

Tolu was shocked but recovered quickly. "I didn't think I would have to see you again either. I had thought it was good riddance to bad rubbish..." she said, giving it back to him.

"Really? Now you're talking, so that was what you thought of me? Tell me more." He said mildly, too mildly.

Tolu continued as if she didn't hear his comment. "And I wasn't expecting to be employed the same day, I only thought you would be kind enough to help, but I guess I was wrong." Tight lipped, Tolu took her bag, and made to get up, since it appeared there was nothing more to be said.

A frown crossed his face, but disappeared as quickly as it had come. "You've changed." Ben said, softening his voice, giving her a deliberate scrutiny.

She didn't like the effect his eyes were having on her, but she tried to remain calm. She looked down at her bag on her laps, and looked up back at him. "Have I? Well, I guess so. People change, and you have changed as well, especially your manners." She replied bluntly, finishing with a smile, to soften the impact of her comment on his manners. She liked to be blunt.

Ben laughed out loud. "Oh - I didn't realize. Anyway you must agree with me it's been a long time, and you were the last person I was expecting to see. Forgive me if I've been a bit cold …"

She cut in, "Not a bit cold, but very cold and rude."

Ben laughed again and continued, "Well if I have been very cold and rude, but your coming is rather a shock."

"You're looking well though." She acknowledged, the smile still on her face.

"Thanks. I didn't realize you were still in Lagos. I thought you might have travelled or something. Do you still live with your parents?"

His voice was now good tempered. Memories flooded his mind, why should he be asking these personal questions, he wondered. Just, trying to be polite, he told himself unconvincingly.

Just then, Kemi came in with a note in her hand to announce the arrival of another visitor. Ben stretched his hand to take the note from her, just as Tolu got up. Ben looked at her questioningly.

"I guess I should be on my way now. Sorry for taking your time."

"Not at all, and I'll see what I can do about the other issue. You can phone next week to know how far." Ben gave her his complimentary card and continued,

"My regards to your family."

"Bye, have a good evening." Tolu replied and went out.

A t least she had tried, Tolu told herself as she got out of the elevator that had taken her from the fifth floor, which occupied Ben's office. She walked out of the building to the street below in a slight daze, still somehow shocked by her meeting with Ben. She didn't expect to be as affected as she was. She had thought it was over between them, and that it would be safe to work with him. Her going to him for a job might not be such a good idea after all.

As she entered a taxi that would take her home, she still thought about their meeting. Did God actually tell her to go and meet him when she prayed concerning finding work? she asked herself, trying to check her spirit, or did she go, led by her own emotions, wanting to take advantage of the relationship she once shared with him? She had expected he would be glad to help. If that was what she wanted to achieve, well it was not working, from the look of things. *Oh God, take control*, she said silently. Maybe she was a fool for going to see him. But then, she was curious about him, she must admit.

She felt a little guilty just then. She knew as a Christian, she should not go to people of the opposite sex for such favours, it would put her in a difficult situation. They had been taught that, several times at the singles fellowship. God was to be her source. She should not try to help God by running to the opposite sex. They would not normally give without expecting something in return. There would be strings attached, except if the man giving the favour is a true Christian. There was a local film she watched on telly, where a girl started sleeping with her uncle all in a bid to have her needs met. Tolu felt troubled and bothered.

What had she done? Probably, she should have *let sleeping dogs lie.*

The taxi pulled up in front of her parents' house, and she got out. The house was the third on that short street, a few buildings away from Yvonne's house. It had a large compound, with beautiful flowers planted all around. The car in the driveway told her that her parents must be around.

As she came into the apartment, her mother looked up from the television. "You're early, when did the fellowship end?" Her mother asked.

"I'm not coming from church. I went to see someone concerning my job." Tolu responded tiredly.

"Oh, how did it go? Although I know God will do the best. He is never late, you know. I'm sure there's a miracle around the corner for you." Mrs. Pratt said, trying to encourage her daughter, because of the sullen look she saw on her face.

Her mother was also a Christian. It was Tolu who got converted first, and then she brought her parents and younger ones to Christ too.

I might as well drop the bomb and see her reaction.

"I went to see Ben."

"Ben who?"

"Ben Wright. He owns a company called Wright Ally Computers and the company is doing well." Tolu said casually, slumping into a chair. As she pulled off her shoes, her mother gave her a searching look.

"Ben Wright? Where did you see him?"

"In his office. I went there."

"So, what happened? Although I doubt if that was the right thing to do, you should not be desperate, although I trust you. You have always been a reasonable and level-headed girl. I always thank God for giving you and your two sisters to me, but you have to be careful, not forgetting about the wiles of Satan."

Trust Mummy - Tolu smiled, "No problem Mum, and to answer your question on what happened – nothing. I don't know if he wants to help. What's there to eat?" Tolu quickly changed the subject, she didn't want to discuss Ben now, and she was glad her mother didn't press the issue. She had had enough of Ben for one day, she thought, as she got up and strolled to the kitchen, bare footed. The kitchen was beyond the dining room and an open stairway leading to the upstairs bedrooms stood on a side.

"There's rice in the pot for you." Mrs. Pratt called after her.

As Tolu served her food, she shouted from the kitchen, "Where's Dad?"

"He's just gone out."

As she ate, she chatted light heartedly with her mother.

Later that night in her room, Tolu turned restlessly on the bed. She hissed and turned yet again, wishing she could sleep. She turned her pillow to the other side, trying to find a cool spot on it, if that would make her sleep. She just couldn't get Ben out of her mind. He looked as handsome as ever, and more in control.

As she thought of him, she experienced a deep sinking feeling in her soul. She turned again, looked upward and sighed. If their relationship had not been cut off by her Mum, who knows, they might be married now, and she would be his wife.

He must be married, she was sure. Someone as successful as that, and with his kind of looks would have no problem finding someone to marry. But he had no wedding ring on, probably he forgot to wear it, *men are like that,* she concluded. His wife must be happy, very fortunate. How she wished she was his wife. N*o no no-Tolu, get real*, she scolded herself. There was no point crying over spilled milk. What happened could not be reversed.

Then she remembered Paul's words in the Bible about forgetting the past.

Anyway, they were no longer together, and she was now a Christian. There was no way she could marry an unbeliever. She gave herself a mental shake. She had passed that stage. She was so sure he could not be a believer. With such handsome looks and money, it was not likely, she concluded.

But why am I thinking like this? She thought broodingly. She felt restless. At this rate, if care was not taken, she wasn't going to sleep tonight at all. She tried to drag her mind to the church, away from Ben, but somehow found her thoughts drifting back.

She hissed yet again, then took her pillow and put it on her head, holding it in place with her two hands, as if to shut out thoughts of Ben. She knew Ben loved her then, when they were together, and it had broken her heart when her mother who was not converted at that time insisted she stopped seeing him, because to her, Ben was not the kind of man she should marry. Ben was a struggling young man at that time who had just started to work. Her mother was a strong woman, and once her mind was made up concerning something, that was it. There was nothing Tolu could do.

There was no point thinking about the past, or what could have been, Tolu advised herself. This was not the time for memories. She glanced at the wall clock, it was midnight. She must get some sleep. She threw back the sheet, got up and swung her feet to the floor. Straightening her night dress in front, she went to the kitchen and prepared a cold beverage drink, if it would help her to relax and sleep.

She brought the drink to the room on a tray, set it on her bedside table and got on the bed again. She brought out a book titled - *God knows* - and started reading, at the same time, sipping her drink.

By the time she finished her drink, she knew what to do. She had to pray. She closed the book and her eyes and started praying, admitting her weakness in the situation, and asking God to direct her path and strengthen her to do His will. While still praying she drifted into an exhausted sleep.

****

Tolu sat on the three-seater with her legs folded in front of her, and her head rested on the back of the settee.

Her eyes were closed, as she thought of so many things. It had been two weeks since that day she went to see Ben, and since then she had not been able to get thoughts of him out of her mind. Not that she still loved him, she convinced herself, but the kind of relationship they shared leaves a residue. It was normal to think of him, and she guessed she could never forget him. Not only was he handsome and intelligent, he was also charming and thoughtful. He was a real friend to her, he believed in her, and treated her like something precious, that should be protected. If she was sad, she ran to him for comfort, and with him she felt safe. Why did she allow her mother to break them up?

Tolu sighed, unwound her legs, stretching them straight before her. Probably she should have done something, but then she knew her mother did what she thought was best for her. Her mother too did not know Christ at the time. She thought Gbenga would be a better partner for Tolu than Ben, and Gbenga, who was ten years older than her and was working in a bank, also came from her town and he did not hide the fact that he found her attractive. They lived in the same neighbourhood, and her mother liked him. Her mother's plan was to break her from Ben and push her to Gbenga, and that was how she found herself dating Gbenga shortly after her break-up with Ben. But the relationship didn't last.

Two months later, she gave her life to Christ, and ended the relationship. Her mother was upset. She tried to tell her she was making a mistake, gave her reasons to remain in the relationship, but eventually gave up when Tolu would not budge. Instead, Tolu started telling her mother about the love of God, and His plans for His children. She was so glad the day her mother followed her to church and prayed the sinner's prayer, surrendering her life to Christ.

Tolu got up and went to her room. She had not really been herself since the day she saw Ben again in his office. Why?- she could not place the feeling, but it felt like pain. *Sometimes one does not know what one has until it is lost,* she thought.

She changed her dress and wore her shoes. She would go to the salon, anything to take her mind off this man. She left her room, closing the door behind her.

"Moni, I'm off to the salon."

"What did you say?" Moni asked from the bathroom.

"I'm going to Meg's, to fix my hair. I'll be back shortly."

"Okay, jam the door, Bye."

She began to stroll down the road to the salon. A red car approached. The driver flashed the lights of the car at her, and her mind skipped a bit - could it be Ben - coming to see her, after all? The car came close, and she realized it was Yvonne.

The car stopped beside her. "Hi." Yvonne called out excitedly.

"Hi, how are you?"

"Fine, have you been to see Ben?"

"Yeah, I went some days ago."

"Really? So have you started?"

"Started? Not likely."

"Why?" Yvonne frowned her disappointment. "What did he say?"

"Nothing much. He collected my C.V and that was all."

"Really?" The dark complexioned lady said, adjusting her eye glasses. "Let me talk to him."

"No way." Tolu said immediately, "If he does not want to help, it's his choice. He will have his reasons. And how do we know if it is not God that's at work? I don't want you to go and beg him on my behalf."

"It won't be begging, I will just make him see reason ..."

Tolu shook her head, "No, don't. Let's not force issues."

Yvonne didn't agree. She would find a way to see Ben. She sighed and changed the subject. "Where are you going?"

"I'm going to the salon." She pointed towards the place.

"Okay, have a nice day."

"You too, bye."

I don't want anyone to try to persuade him - Tolu told herself defiantly, as she resumed her walk towards the salon. If he wanted to help he would have been in touch.

****

Ben gestured towards a chair, "Yvonne, please sit down. Kemi where's the letter?"

The lady blinked, looking a bit confused. "I thought ..."

"Please stop thinking, and use your head." Ben snapped, cutting her off.

Kemi smiled, and left for the adjoining office.

Yvonne frowned at him.

Kemi soon came back with some papers.

"What about Mr Ojo's address?"

Kemi rolled her eyes upward. "I don't know the address."

"You've been there twice, Kemi. I have to see the man this evening, unfailingly. Where does he live?"

"Ikeja."

"Where in Ikeja?"

"I think - I think the street is Ma – something. It's close to maybe..." She frowned, "It's close to Sho - something." She offered timidly.

"Very good. I think Ma something, close to may be Sho - something. Look Kemi, you have to wake up! These days you're getting on my nerves." Ben scowled.

Kemi burst out into laughter.

Yvonne who had been listening to them, now looked from one to the other, wondering what was going on.

Ben frowned, "And what's so funny?"

When her laughter subsided a little she told him, "Recently, you've been irritable and snappy, which is unlike you, and the way you go on - it's just amusing to me." She laughed again.

Ben gave her a long look, "Well I'm not laughing because I don't see what's amusing you. Where in Ikeja does he live?"

Kemi muttered something.

"What?"

"I said it's like you started from the day that lady came in the evening." Kemi spoke clearly.

"Wha...? Tolu?"

"I don't know her name. She came about two weeks ago." She didn't mince words.

Yvonne looked at Ben, "Tolu Pratt?"

Ben looked at Yvonne as if to say something but changed his mind, and turned to Kemi, staring at her.

"I can take you there," The secretary offered.

"Write down the direction and let me have it."

"Okay." Kemi left.

Yvonne leaned forward, "Ben..."

Ben raised his hands up, "I don't want to talk about it."

"No way. It's because of her I've come."

"Yeah, I've forgotten you told her to come. Thanks a lot." Ben said sarcastically.

"My pleasure," Yvonne laughed. "How would I know her coming would affect you so much?"

He denied it quickly, "It's not affecting me."

Yvonne put her bag down on the chair beside her, and sat forward. "You should convince yourself about that, not me. When is Tolu resuming?" Because of their close relationship, she could ask him for such favour.

Ben laughed. "Look Yvonne..."

"You've not answered me." She was determined to achieve what she came for.

Ben looked at her. They had known each other from elementary school. She was about the same age with him and unmarried as well.

Ben looked away, "It's not that easy Yvonne." He explained, his elbows were on the arms of his chair.

"Why not, Ben?"

When Ben didn't respond, she asked, "Because of your association with her in the past? See it as helping someone."

Ben looked down at the table. "You won't understand."

"You're right, I won't. I don't see how you will be in a position to help and you won't."

"I have not said I won't employ her. That's not the problem." Ben said with a tinge of annoyance. "Try to understand."

"I've already told you I can't understand why not."

"Too bad." Ben was clearly irritated now as he got up to stand by the window.

He pulled the blinds to a side and looked out. "How can I have her work with me? What if we get attracted to each other again?"

"Let's look at it this way. She can be transferred to the other company."

He turned to face her, hands in pockets. "I'll give it a thought. Any other thing?"

"Are you telling me you hate her so much that you're dismissing..."

"I don't hate her. How can I?"

"You love her?" Yvonne raised her brows questioningly.

Ben walked back to his seat. "This is not a joking matter, Yvonne. She is out of my life."

She picked the newspaper on his table. "Think about it. Aren't you going to offer me something?"

"With all the harassment, you don't deserve anything." Ben told her jokingly.

Yvonne smiled, crossing an ankle over the other. "Now, be a good boy."

Ben dialed the intercom. "Kemi, please come."

****

Ben bent his head over the scatter of papers on his table for some minutes. With a sigh he looked up, packed the papers together and set them aside. He sat back on the chair and poured himself some coffee. The particular day Tolu came, he had a bad night. He couldn't sleep. He kept remembering her visit. Her face kept haunting him, and he didn't know why.

For a long time, he replayed her visit to his office and what transpired between them in his memory. He recalled her smile, her dressing, the look of agitation on her face, what she said and his own reply. He thought about her comment on his cold attitude, and blamed himself. Maybe he should have behaved differently. He also remembered the way she bit her lips. She used to do that whenever she was nervous.

Flashing back in his mind to the experiences he had shared with Tolu filled his heart with a sense of warmth tinged with pain. To take his mind off, he had read late into the night, and then turned on the telly just to prevent himself from thinking.

For a while, he concentrated on the television, following the program, but not for long. In fact, he didn't realize his thoughts had drifted back to Tolu immediately until a noise in the television jolted him back to reality.

Coming back to the present, he still had not decided if he should employ her. He had prayed, asking God to tell him what to do. He knew he was still bitter and resentful and that was unbecoming of a Christian. He remembered a message he had heard preached on disappointments. Yes, he was disappointed and it still hurt, but he learnt from the message that if disappointment was not handled the right way, it could lead to bitterness and unforgiveness, and the person could end up destroying himself.

The negative emotion of bitterness and pain he felt was alien to him. He had thought nobody and nothing could hurt or make him get disturbed, but what he was experiencing now, shocked him. He should not react to her this way, like some kid having a crush on a lady.

His mind went back to that moment six years ago. Her mother in particular had been very insulting, telling him to stay away from Tolu as she would not be allowed to marry a man from Abeokuta, and definitely not Ben, as he was not her kind of son-in-law. She had said a lot of things to him that he still remembered. Tolu had not appeared to be taking side with her mother though, but she didn't say much either. She just looked confused. He had looked at her, expecting her to say something, and he had tried to convince Mrs. Pratt, telling her he would make it one day, and that he truly loved her daughter, Tolu. He had said a lot of things in a bid to save the situation, but had to leave when he realized Mrs. Pratt had made up her mind to separate them. She must have hated him. He kept writing letters to Tolu, and twice, he sent friends to discuss with her, but there was never a reply from her, and eventually, he too stopped. He was disappointed and shattered.

Something told him he should employ her as Yvonne had said, and not think too much of it, but on the other hand, he didn't want to, if only to prove a point to her and Mrs. Pratt that he had made it after all, and he was still the same person from Abeokuta. He wanted his own pound of flesh.

Ben sipped his coffee, as he thought of taking his pound of flesh. Gently, a voice spoke to him to trust in the Lord with all his heart and not lean on his own understanding. He heaved a heavy sigh and shook his head. Well, he guessed he must do the right thing. And if he was to employ her, he might as well do it without delay. There was no point in hanging about, he decided, but he would keep her at an arm's length.

He brought out Tolu's C. V. from where he had put it two weeks ago, wrote her name and address on a sheet of paper and called his secretary.

"Call me Udoh," he said curtly, with his head bent down writing a note to Tolu.

The secretary left and about five minutes later, Udoh came in.

"You sent for me sir?" he asked politely, with his two hands linked behind him.

"Take this note to this address and tell her to see me tomorrow. The driver will take you there."

"Yes sir." Udoh replied taking the note from Ben.

God I'm doing this because I believe you want me to help her - Ben told God, under his breath. *Let it not turn out to be a mistake* - he prayed.

CHAPTER
THREE

Tolu was not at home when the note was delivered. She had gone to see a friend, and from there headed to church for the mid week service. She had agreed with her mother to meet her and her sisters in church at six. The service ended at half past seven.

She had enjoyed the service that evening, and was especially blessed by the song rendered by the choir. She still remembered the song, and was singing it as their car came to a halt in front of the house - *we may not know how, we may not know when, but He'll do it again.*

The song had ministered to her and she regarded it as God's words to her. Could it be that God was about to perform a miracle in her life? A voice told her there was no miracle coming her way, they were just words of a song, a beautiful song, but that was all, she should not read meanings to it. But another voice told her she should claim the message of the song, and not regard it as a mere song, because it would be to her according to her faith. This latter voice quickly added *"remember God says His thoughts toward you are thoughts of good and not evil."*

That is it - Tolu said, smiling, "God let it be to me

according to your word, I choose to believe you. I know you will not fail nor forsake me in Jesus' name."

She came into the flat with her mother and sisters and they greeted Mr. Pratt.

"How was service today?" asked Mr. Pratt.

"Wonderful!"

"Glory to God!"

While the others chatted, Tolu went to her room to change and soon came back to join them in the sitting room.

"Tolu, someone brought a note for you this morning from Wright Ally Computers Company, and said you should be there tomorrow to see the Managing Director."Her father informed her.

"A note from Wright Ally?" She repeated, her heart beginning to race, as she took the note from her father.

She looked at the handwriting. It was unmistakably Ben's. She would recognize it anywhere. She tore it open immediately, and brought out the sheet of paper inside, it read - *Come tomorrow at about ten, ask for Mr. Adeogba, he will interview you- Signed Ben.*

Emotions surged through her. She wasn't expecting it to be quite like this, *Oh my God, should I go there?* She quickly sat down with the note still in her hand.

Her mother had noticed her reaction. *Wright Ally Computers* - was that not Ben's company?

"Is that from Ben?" her mother asked quietly.

"Yes, he wants me to come tomorrow for an interview." Tolu supplied.

"Hmm." Mrs. Pratt said as she went to the kitchen.

"That's nice." Moni said, taking the note from Tolu, as she joined her on the settee.

"Is he married?"

"I don't know. Why?"

"Nothing. Where's his office?"

"Victoria Island."

"Do I know the Ben?" Mr. Pratt questioned.

"It's Ben. Ben Wright." Tolu replied, sure the name would ring a bell in her father's mind.

Everyone knew them together, they were like a snail and its shell.

Mr. Pratt remembered. "Oh - I didn't realize you still kept in touch. What's he in to?" Her father asked.

"I didn't keep in touch. I saw him just some days ago, and told him I was looking for a job. The company deals in sales of computers."

Mrs. Pratt came to the sitting room, "Thank God for that. Is he now married?"

"Why is everyone asking me if he's married? He has only asked me to come for an interview, not to marry him." She narrowed her eyes at her mother.

"Who else has asked you? Moni?" All of them burst into laughter.

After the evening's family devotion, which was led by Mr. Pratt, before Tolu went to her room, her mother asked her. "Are you going there tomorrow?"

"I guess I have to." Tolu answered, "Any objections?"

Mrs. Pratt put a hand round her first daughter's shoulders sympathetically, "Well, I'm just wondering if it's a good idea to work for him, considering the fact that you used to go out together. You lost contact for over six years, and you met him just some days ago." Mrs. Pratt stopped.

Tolu raised an eyebrow, tongue in cheek. "Are you sure your doubt is really because we met only some days ago and not because he is a man from Abeokuta?"

Mrs. Pratt smiled, she knew Tolu was just teasing.

"Really, I used to believe men from that place wouldn't make good husbands, that they would make life unbearable for their wives. That is what I believed, but I know better now. You can marry a man from anywhere. Do whatever you feel God is leading you to do, but maintain your integrity." With that Mrs. Pratt left the room.

****

The following morning, she put on a yellow skirt suit, which was one of her favourite wears, and a green silk camisole. She slipped on her yellow shoes and round her waist was a golden belt. She styled her hair and she was set. She carried her black leather bag, and checked herself in the mirror. What she saw pleased her, and she left, wishing herself the very best.

When she got to Wright Ally, she decided to see Ben first, so she approached the secretary.

"Mr. Wright is on the phone. You won't be able to see him now," Kemi told her, giving her a friendly smile.

"Oh - can I see Mr. Adeogba then? He's expecting me."

"He's on the 4th floor."

Tolu thanked her, and proceeded promptly to

Mr. Adeogba's office. It appeared Mr. Adeogba had given certain instructions to the receptionist on his floor, because she was ushered in immediately.

Mr. Adeogba was a dark complexioned man, in his mid thirties, and of an average height. When he saw Tolu, he got up, shook hands with her and sat down again, indicating for Tolu to take her seat. He appeared to be a busy man because he promptly requested for her credentials and started to interview her.

Within twenty minutes he was through with the interview, and told her to wait for her letter of employment. He scribbled some things on a paper and went to the adjoining room to discuss with his secretary. He came back to his office.

"Your letter will soon be ready. Just five minutes."

"That is okay," Tolu nodded.

Wright Ally must be a fairly big company to occupy two floors and have a man like Mr. Adeogba in its employment. And from the look of things the number of staff cannot be less than twenty, Tolu thought as she looked round the room. Soon, someone pushed open the door and a lady came in.

"Oh it's ready. Thank you."

"Yes sir." The lady handed over the letter to Mr. Adeogba and left.

He read through it, and signed. He gave the letter to Tolu informing her she would be expected to resume work on Monday as an Accountant.

Tolu thanked him and got out. She wondered if Ben would have finished his telephone conversation. She hesitated a little, using her right hand to straighten her skirt, and then headed for Ben's office.

Don't worry about a thing, she tried to calm herself, as the secretary waved her through.

There was a pile of papers on the table, and he had his head bent, checking them. Without looking up, Ben said, "Kemi, get me Chrislink on phone."

Tolu quickly responded, "It's me. Shall I call the secretary for you?"

Ben lifted his head sharply, "Good morning Tolu. Please call her for me."

Tolu went back and soon came in again with the secretary behind her.

"Tolu have your sit. Kemi please get me Chrislink right away."

"Alright sir," Kemi went out, but not before giving Ben a knowing wink, which he ignored.

He bent his head back to the paper and asked, "Have you seen Mr. Adeogba?"

"Yes and I just want to thank you Ben, or maybe I should say Mr. Wright, since I'll be working for you now. Thank you very much." She concluded with a smile.

"That's alright. I wish you a nice time with us." Ben said, sounding as if he was dismissing her.

Tolu jumped to her feet, "That's all. Don't let me take your time. Thank you very much Mr. Wright."

Mr. Wright! Very good. He preferred it that way. No closeness.

****

When Tolu resumed on Monday, she thought of going to Ben's office, when she was less busy, to let him know she had resumed, and to once again show her appreciation, but she thought against it immediately. He was so formally cold towards her, and behaved as if he wouldn't want to be disturbed.

In the evening, at home, Moni came to her room.

"Hi, how did it go today?"

"I survived as you can see."

Moni's expression suddenly brightened, "So, is he married?"

She frowned, "Moni, what's your problem? Why are you asking me if he's married?"

The slender lady shrugged, looking put out. "I thought you would know."

"How would I know? And why should I?" Tolu asked, her tone tight.

"You could have found out."

Tolu looked at her sister and burst into laughter. "Mo-o-ni! Well, I don't know, and it's none of my business."

"Aren't you interested?" Moni continued stubbornly.

"No-o-o." She replied coolly.

"Well, that's where we are different."

Tolu's eyes widened with disapproval, "Mo-o-ni! See how you're talking, like someone who doesn't have the Holy Spirit in her."

Moni shrugged, "Look, one has to be wise. How old are you now, twenty seven ...."

Tolu breathed in heavily, "I don't need that sort of wisdom,

Moni. I prefer to go on with God. God's foolishness is wiser than men. And Moni, I don't know if you're trying to be funny, but I don't find what you're saying funny. Look at you, dating Fred..."

Moni raised a hand up, "Please let's not talk about Fred. Keep your advice."

Tolu yawned, covering her mouth with the back of her hand. She got on the bed.

Moni didn't like the way she was being dismissed, "I'm as much a Christian as you are."

Tolu laughed, "You don't even have a choice other than to be one." She said, as she got under the sheet.

****

Throughout the week, Tolu didn't see Ben, and she was beginning to feel uneasy about it. He might not even know she had resumed.

She began to blame herself. She should actually go to see him, courtesy demanded it, she reasoned with a grimace.

Eventually she summoned up courage on friday and went to see him.

When she entered Ben's office, he was standing, obviously getting ready to go out. He looked up as she entered.

"Good afternoon Mr. Wright," she said, her gaze meeting his. If he preferred to be formal, it was alright by her. She could be formal too.

Ben raised his brows and looked at her consideringly,

She has not forgotten to call me Mr. Wright. Good, he liked that. But what he felt was pain. Pain that she had pushed him out of her mind and life.

But with a soft smile to cover up, he asked, "How are you?"

"I'm fine." Tolu drawled and then quickly plunged into what she had to say before he dismissed her. "I just thought I should let you know I've resumed since Monday. I would have come, but didn't want to disturb you."

"I know, Mr. Adeogba briefed me. How are you getting on though?" Ben said smoothly. "Have your seat." He added softly, his eyes taking in her dressing.

She looked as beautiful as ever. Tolu was wearing a pure silk red dress with a black jacket and scarf thrown on her left shoulder. Her dark long hair was neatly packed in a lovely way and she had her feet in red high heeled shoes.

"I wonder if I can have a P. C. system in my office to work with?"

Ben rested his back and breathed in. "I've actually wanted to see you. I've been discussing with Mr. Adeogba about the possibility of posting you to another place. There's this other company - Wright Investments - it's a sister company. It took off some months ago, and we're trying to put some things in place. I'm thinking of your being there to manage it. There are seven people there. The office is just two streets away from here. If you go out of this building to the road, turn left, then take the first turning on the right. You go straight down till you get to a brown building. The road that turns off that building is it. Brigg's street, number 13."

"What's the company into?"

"It's a trading company. There's a guy who has been

going from here to that place to oversee the staff. His name is Lekan. You'll liaise with him. He will take you there, introduce you to the other staff, and you may ask him for whatever you need."

Ben dialed the intercom, "Lekan, please come."

While waiting for Lekan, Ben asked, "How is your family?"

"Everyone is fine, thank you. And yours?"

"They're okay."

"Actually my parents send their greetings.Mum in particular would like to thank you specially. She wanted to come over, but I told her not to bother, that I would convey her message." She stopped to clear her throat. "This Wright Investments, will you want me to go there today?"

Ben shrugged, "It depends, but the earlier the better."

Just then, Lekan knocked and entered.

"Good day Ben, Tolu how are you?" Lekan patted Tolu briefly on the shoulder, as he took his seat.

"I can see you two have met already, fast work."

Fast work? Tolu looked from him to Lekan and back. What did he mean? Lekan just smiled. He didn't seem to read any meaning to it.

"Miss Pratt is going to head Wright Investments." Ben continued innocently. "I've told her you have been overseeing the place, so I'll want you to liaise with her, take her there, probably today or tomorrow at the latest. Acquaint her with the nature of the business, and hand over the books, files and all."

He turned to Tolu, "You will use my office over there as

your office." Then to Lekan, "Lekan, open my office for her. That's where she will be, and make sure she has all she needs. Right?"

"Alright." Lekan answered, then turned at an angle to face Tolu, "I'll come to your office, so we can go. Give me about thirty minutes," he got up, and Tolu followed.

About an hour later, Tolu left with Lekan in his car to Wright Investments office.

As Tolu got down, she considered the surrounding and the building. It was a two-storey ash coloured building, with tiled ground.

Cars were parked in front and inside, with beautiful flowers planted all around. The signboard of Wright Investments stood in front of the building.

They entered the building through swing doors, and progressed along a carpeted corridor to the reception.

"Mr. Lekan, good afternoon, *e ku ijo meta*," the elegant receptionist greeted him.

" Mercy, *how are you, ewo le se?*"

" *I dey your side o.* Good afternoon madam," Mercy acknowledged Tolu.

" Good afternoon, how are you? I'm Tolu Pratt." Tolu shot out her hand, for a handshake which Mercy acknowledged.

Lekan introduced Tolu to other people and moved inside the main office. Tolu followed. There was a big general office, and four doors, leading to rooms.

Lekan greeted the people there before proceeding to a door. He knocked and entered with Tolu.

"Chucks how are you?" Lekan called out cheerfully.

The dark complexioned man with tribal marks on his face stood up and shook hands with him, then he turned to Tolu, " Good day Madam,"

Tolu smiled at him, "Good day Mr. Chucks, how is everything?"

" Fine thank you, please sit down,"

They did and Lekan proceeded promptly to explain the presence of Tolu. Some minutes later, the three of them got up and went to the room Ben used as his office in Wright Investments.

Some files were on the glass table in the room, a P.C., and a pen holder. Some paintings and a clock hung on the cream coloured wall.

"This will be your office, and this," Lekan pointed at a door inside the room, "is the toilet." He opened a cabinet and brought out files, ledgers, vouchers and some loose sheets.

Three visitors chairs were set in front of the glass table. They pulled the chairs and sat down to discuss and intimate Tolu with the company she would begin to manage.

****

Ben kept away from her, fighting the urge to see her, reminding himself he didn't have to see her, and he must keep to his resolution to distance himself. But by the end of the week, he convinced himself he should go to Wright Investments, at least to know what was going on.

Tolu was picking up her bag, about to go out for lunch when her door opened and in came Ben.

Surprised, she said, " Good afternoon Mr. Wright," her heart beating rapidly as it always did at the sight of him.

"Miss Pratt," Ben said, with a smile, "I just wanted to see how you're faring. How are you?" He said, sitting on one of the visitors' chairs.

"I'm okay as you can see." She answered.

Ben was still looking round her table when suddenly his gaze fell on a black leather Bible and some audio tapes beside the cassette player on one side of her table.

No, it couldn't be! "Is that Bible yours?" He enquired from beneath raised eyebrows.

Tolu, who was sitting down opposite him, looked at the object he was referring to, and a sudden wave of panic surged through her.

With carefulness, not really knowing what he thought of a Bible, or what his reaction might be, she said, "Yes,"

"Which church do you attend?" Ben probed further.

" *Praise to our King Chapel,* " she would have given anything to know what he was thinking.

Really? He had some friends in that church. Was she a Christian? Ben wondered. "Are you a believer?" he asked further still.

The word *believer* struck her, and the way he used it. Not so many people used it. Could he be a believer himself? Not likely, Tolu thought, especially with his rare combination of looks, wealth, and brains.

"Yes," her stomach clenched. Why was Ben asking all these questions?

Ben got up abruptly and went round the table to where

the tapes were. Picking them up one by one and examining he asked, "Since when?"

It was now obvious to Tolu that he was trying to discover something. "It will be five years in February," Tolu replied, wondering why all these questions.

Ben was silent. It was around that time that he gave his life to Christ at a program he was invited to in Ibadan. He could not forget that day. He was still brooding, feeling terribly disturbed over his broken relationship with Tolu and he had agreed to attend the program with a friend, just to take his mind off his problem. He was never a drinker nor a smoker, he could have just turned to that. Just to while away time, Ben had followed his friend. He expected it would be boring, but the program turned out to be very interesting.

There was a drama, then the choir sang, and the climax was the message delivered by the Pastor titled - *The cloud of glory.*

Ben had sat glued to his chair, his eyes moving to and fro with the movement of that pastor. He was surprised to see himself laughing and clapping with the congregation and when the call was made, Ben came out, giving his life to Christ. When it was time for offering, and they started singing praise songs, he jumped up dancing, as if he had been doing it all his life. Since then, his life had never been the same again.

Ben smiled, still holding and turning the audio tapes over in his hands. The smile made Tolu's heart skip a beat. His smile was one of the many things that had endeared him to her, and she suddenly realized she had missed the smile all the years they had been separated. She wished he would smile again, but she quickly dismissed the thought and tried to bring her mind to more neutral ground - the audio tapes - the reason for all those questions.

She decided to ask him, "May I know why you're asking me all these questions?"

"Um - let's just say curiosity, I'll be going now. If there's need to see me, you can always call, or come around. Next week, let's say Friday, I'd like you to bring the bank schedules, the debtors accounts as well as creditors accounts over to Wright Ally. I'd like to know our balances. On the debtors, separate the corporate customers from individuals and extract the balances. I'll expect you in the afternoon, Friday next week. Have a nice day." And with that, Ben strode out briskly, letting the door slowly close, leaving Tolu in a mixture of feelings.

CHAPTER
FOUR

Why was he asking her all those questions about her faith? Had he been told something about her, that made him come to her office to check for himself? The thought made her shudder. It must be Mr. Adeogba, she concluded.

She remembered that Mr. Adeogba came to her office when she was at Wright Ally, as she was witnessing to one of the girls in the office who had become friendly. They did not set out to talk about Jesus, the discussion had just got round to church and she felt it was an opportunity to make her know of the love of Jesus. But she could still recollect the look of surprise Mr. Adeogba displayed when he realized what was being discussed. Yes, Ben must have got wind of it.

But, he didn't look annoyed - Tolu thought. And there was no way she could have denied when he asked her about her church. She didn't deny Christ all these years, and she wasn't about to deny Him now. But what would Ben think of her?

Tolu frowned and hissed. But why was she so bothered what he thought of her, afterall they were strangers now, weren't they? And she was not interested in him. or was she?

She sat back on her chair, with her head between her hands.

There was a gentle knock on her door, and Nike, the girl she had witnessed to at Wright Ally strolled in.

"Tolu, are you not going on break?" she asked brightly.

"I don't think so. How are you Nike?" Tolu said quietly.

"Fine, but that's more than I can say for you." Nike remarked, staring at Tolu with probing eyes, "You don't look your normal cheerful self. What's the matter?" Nike asked with a look of concern, coming closer to Tolu, all the while watching her.

"Nothing, don't mind me." Tolu forced a smile, "Where are you going for lunch?" she asked trying to sound cheerful.

"I'm not going yet. I'm waiting for Josiah. We plan to go shopping for some things we'll need for our wedding. I told him to meet me here. We still have quite a lot to do, and the wedding is just a month away." Nike explained throwing her hands up in the air.

"Where is the wedding taking place, Lagos or Josiah's hometown?" Tolu asked with interest.

"It's here in Lagos. Most of his people are based here in Lagos, and of course, I am a Lagosian."

"Hmm, I'm happy for you. And you're so fortunate to be getting married to a man who adores you." Tolu commented.

"Oh yeah, I'm fortunate, ain't I?" Then giving Tolu a straight look, Nike asked, "What about you, when are you getting married? Is he someone in your church?"

How do I answer that, Tolu asked herself and with a chuckle, she answered, "Don't worry, at the right time, you'll be informed, is that okay?"

"Tolu babe, eh-I know you can't have problem finding a suitable man. Men in your church *go just dey die* for you." Nike said, shaking Tolu's hand.

Tolu laughed and told Nike mockingly. "They don't die in my church o, God forbid. Anyway, em, it's not really like that. Someone has to pray, and then trust God to work things out." Tolu explained.

"How should the person pray, and how does one trust God to work things out ?" Nike was serious now.

Tolu smiled again. She knew Nike would ask. "How do I explain it? To pray, the man or woman will tell God to lead him or her to the right person, that will be suitable for him or her. And on how to trust God to work things out, the first point is - you don't know everything about your potential partner, and you don't know lots of things about yourself. And so you can't guess the future. God is all-knowing. He knows what you need, and who fits you. So when the person meets someone, he or she has to pray, think, talk with the person to know him or her better, and apply the wisdom contained in the word of God and see how the potential partner measures up. If the person has prayed, then he or she must trust God that he won't make a mistake as the Spirit of God will guide him or her. Do you understand, or have I confused you?" Tolu chuckled.

"I understand. But for someone like me who is getting married soon and hasn't actually prayed about the relationship, what do you think I should do?"

"Well, all you have to do is talk to God about the relationship and ask Him for His help and guidance even as you're preparing for the wedding. And don't forget to commit your fiance into His hands. After praying to God first, then you call your fiance and discuss with him about the need for the two of you to get closer to God. But most importantly, you need to give your life to Jesus because God says anyone who does not have His Spirit is not His. If you become a child of God, it will be easy for you to hear and be guided by God...."

Just then, someone knocked. Tolu and Nike looked up at the door.

Tolu quickly chipped in, "You can still pray to God about it ." Then raising her voice, she asked, "Yes, who is it?"

The door opened to a tall young man, wearing a native dress with a cap to match. Nike promptly walked to him and, holding his right hand, she introduced him.

"Tolu, this is my fiance Josiah. Josiah meet Tolu my friend. She joined the company recently."

Tolu stood up and shook hands with Josiah. "It's nice meeting you. Nike has told me about you."

Josiah smiled. "Nice meeting you too.

Taking Josiah's hand with her left hand and using the right one to wave to Tolu, Nike said, "We have to rush along now , so as to get back on time. See ya."

"Have a nice time." Tolu bid them.

****

On Friday, Tolu quickly got dressed up taking extra care with her looks.

"Mum, I'm off." She called to her mother, who

was still in her room.

"Bye, Remember to wait for me in your office, when I finish with Mrs. Adekunle I'll come to pick you."

"When are you supposed to meet Mrs. Adekunle?" Tolu opened the door a little, and poked her head in.

"Three O clock."

"I'll expect you then, I hope you will come on time."

"Bye - have a nice day," said Mrs. Pratt.

****

Ben phoned to remind her of their meeting in the afternoon as if she could forget.

The day proved to be a busy one for her. She continued to gather the information Ben needed together and by noon she was through, running off the statements on the system. At some minutes past three, there was a knock, and Mrs. Pratt came in.

"Hi Mum, you're right on time." She stood up and greeted her mother enthusiastically.

"How are you? How has your day been?"

"Oh it's been busy, but I'm coping. What did Mrs. Adekunle say about the goods?"

Mrs. Pratt explained her discussions with her friend and suddenly stopped to ask. "What about Ben? Will he be in his office?"

"Probably, why?" Tolu queried her mother with a narrowed look.

"I think I should greet and thank him for employing you."

"I think it's not necessary, Ben is a busy man." Tolu tried

to discourage her mother.

   She didn't want Mrs. Pratt to meet Ben yet, not knowing how Ben might react or treat her, after what her mother did six years ago.

   Mrs Pratt stood up. "I think it is necessary, courtesy demands it. Can you take me to his office?"

   Reluctantly Tolu obliged. "I should actually see him too. I'm supposed to have a meeting with him. Is the car outside?"

   "Of course." They left for Wright Ally.

   "Is Mr. Wright in?" She asked Ben's secretary as she entered the office with her mother.

   "Yes," Kemi answered calmly, smiling.

   Tolu cleared her throat, "I have a meeting with him and this is my mother. She wants to see him too."

   "Just a minute please," Kemi said, picking up the phone to inform her boss.

   The telephone on Ben's table shrilled. Picking it up, he asked "What is it Kemi, I'm busy."

   "I'm sorry Ben, but Miss Pratt is here with her mother to see you."

   "With her mother?" *Impossible. What's she doing here,* Ben wondered, clearly surprised.

   "Okay let them in." He braced himself for the meeting with Tolu's mother.

   Tolu knocked on his door and went in, with her mother following.

   He had loosened his tie, which gave him an appealing look. Ben stood up immediately they came in and greeted Tolu's mother, sounding respectful, with no trace of the emotions he felt being revealed.

"Good afternoon ma, *e ku ijo meta ma.*"

"*How are you Ben? Eku ijo meta. Se ise nlo?*"

"*A dupe ma.* Please sit down," Ben said, indicating the chair, and smiled at Tolu.

Tolu and her mother sat down.

"What do I offer you ma? Tea, coffee, soft drink or malt."

"No no no. Don't worry thanks. I came to this area to see a friend and decided to seize the opportunity to pop in and thank you for employing Tolu. She told me everything, how she came and all that. Thank you very much. *A dupe o. Owo a ma roke.* God will continue to bless and prosper you in Jesus' name." Tolu's mother prayed, to which Ben responded with "Amen"

Mrs. Pratt got up."I must be going now, I just wanted to say hello and thank you." Ben stood up too and made to see them out.

"The accounts are on the table, I'll just see my mum out," Tolu said, "I'll be back in a minute," speaking for the first time since they came in.

Ben nodded in agreement and followed them to his secretary's office, before turning back.

Some ten minutes later, Tolu knocked and entered Ben's office. She was about to sit down when he asked,

"Has your mother gone?"

"No she's in Nike's office. She's waiting till I close, so she can give me a ride in her car." Tolu explained.

Ben cast an impatient glance at his watch and said tersely, "She may have to leave without you."

Tolu's mouth dropped open, wondering why.

He continued, "I'll drop you if I have to. We have to sort out these accounts and we may not finish early. I have questions to ask on some of them such as Gross Consults, Linkage Communication. We have to get them ready today because I'll need them at the meeting I'm attending on monday morning." He spoke softly, but his voice was clearly authoritative and Tolu was left in no doubt that he expected her to obey him.

What was she to do? Her mother was waiting so they could go together, and here was Ben saying they might not finish early.

She looked at Ben again with a confused stare. He returned her gaze, with a look that told her he was expecting her answer. What could she do? She would have to go and explain to her mother. She hoped that she would understand.

After what seemed like an endless silence, she said, "I - let me go and tell her. I'll be back soon." Tolu said, hoping Ben was not annoyed that it took her a minute or so to make up her mind. She turned and went.

You don't need to worry. Tolu told herself, on her way back to Ben's office, after discharging her mother. His secretary would be around, definitely. She wouldn't leave with her boss still working in the office. Why was she bothered about being alone, working with him anyway? He definitely was no longer interested in her romantically, anymore than she was, but surprisingly, what she felt was far from being good, it was disappointment.

Breathing heavily, she opened the secretary's office and saw she was coming towards the door.

"Are you off?" Tolu asked.

"Not yet, I'm going to the ladies."

Good. She would be around until they finished - Tolu thought as she entered Ben's office.

He looked up from the papers he had been studying.

"I've been waiting for you, please take your seat and let's go over these."

As Tolu sat down, he started grilling her on the accounts she had prepared, asking questions and jotting down some points.

Some minutes later, he sat back on his chair, dropped the pen in his hand, and with a sigh, he picked the telephone receiver and called his secretary to come.

"Give me a bottle of malt, and em-Tolu, what will you like, is it still coke?" he asked her half mockingly.

Is it still coke? How could he refer to their past together when she had been trying desperately to forget.

Tightlipped she said, "Nothing for me, thanks," she snapped with some irritation.

"Coke for her." Ben said to his secretary, ignoring what Tolu said.

"She's working late today and you can have a bottle for yourself too. You will stay around until she finishes. You're not going yet."

"That's alright, Ben." Kemi said, before leaving to get the drinks.

"Well, if we have to go through these papers today, I suggest we continue. This coke you're asking for is a waste of precious time."

Ben looked at her but made no moves to continue with the accounts, while Tolu remained silent on her seat, with tightened lips and a frown. She sensed he was still looking at her, and to prevent herself from finding out, she picked one of the sheets of accounts from the table and held it up to cover her face, pretending to be reading it even though her mind was not concentrating.

"Can we have biscuits also?" Ben asked the secretary as she came in, placing a tray holding the drinks and glass cups on the table in front of them. She left again to get the biscuits.

Ben picked up the opener and opened the bottles, "I wonder what's wrong with you now, your mood has suddenly changed," he told her perceptively as he poured coke in the cup for her. He pushed the bottle and the cup to Tolu.

"I really don't want it, Mr. Wright. I'm okay." She said trying to control her voice.

"I've opened it already, so you must not let it waste."

Who is he to tell me what I must do? Well I won't drink it, she thought decisively.

The secretary came in with the biscuits on a plate.

"Thank you Kemi. Hang around in your office. If I need you, I'll call."

"No problem sir," Kemi said aloud but in her heart there was a little problem. It happened to be her first child's birthday, and she wouldn't want to get home after he had slept, as she had promised the child a gift. But she couldn't complain since it wasn't often Ben asked her to stay late. She also realized today's overtime was a special case. It was because Tolu was working with him. Nevertheless, Kemi prayed silently that they should be through on time.

"I'll be in the office." Kemi added before going out of Ben's office.

Tolu put the paper down. "Really Mr. Wright, I'll like to leave as soon as possible, can we continue now you've got the drink and biscuits or is there something else you want?"

"What else do you think I may want?"

Tolu had no answer for that.

Ben continued, "Tolu, we're working. I stopped only so we could have drink and biscuits. I've been so busy today, that I could not have my lunch, so it's not as if I intentionally set out to waste your time or that I desire your company for that matter. My asking you to drink is just a matter of courtesy. Alright? So drink your coke and be a good girl."

She felt like saying no, but instead she picked the paper she dropped again and continued to look at it. *Let him tell me when he's ready to continue with the account, as for the coke, he can do whatever he likes with it.*

Ben sipped his drink, putting the cup down, he spoke again. "You really surprise me with the change in your mood. I think it's better to have it out in the open."

He paused and continued, "Is it because you're alone with me? I guess you already know you're in no danger. My secretary is still around, as well as a host of other staff. Besides, you should also know that forcing a woman is not in my repertoire. I'm not that kind. Does that put your mind at rest?"

"I'm not annoyed, and I'm not afraid." Tolu said,

tightlipped. And the part of not being afraid was actually true. She knew Ben very well, at least she used to know him very well and from what she could remember, he was not the kind of bad guy that could force.

"You seem to have forgotten I could read your moods very well in those days, and I think I still know you to some extent." Ben told her.

Why was he taking her down memory lane when she was praying and fighting to forget her past with him?

"There is nothing. I'm just waiting for you so we can conclude on these accounts. I'd like to get home on time if you don't mind."

"We're not continuing until you tell me why you're rude and frowning like this." Ben said.

What? She looked at him with incredulity. *Why is he behaving as if he still cares about me!*

"But Mr. Wright, I don't see how my mood affects the statements I've already prepared." She said with a controlled voice.

"I'm waiting to hear you,"

I'd better say something to get off the hook, Tolu thought. "Well, I guess I am just upset a little and maybe tired as well. I'm sorry if it bothers you, my Lord." She said rudely.

"I still insist." Ben ignored her rudeness.

Now ever so agitated she sipped the drink at last.

Picking a biscuit from the plate, Ben commented with a smile playing on his lips, "I wonder why you keep referring to me as Mr. Wright."

"I prefer to call you that. It's your surname is it not?"

He looked at her for a long time. *So much for bothering himself.*

"Well, suit yourself." He dismissed. "If that's what you want." Ben turned to the papers on the table and he was all professionalism again, commenting on the accounts.

It was about five minutes to seven when they finally finished.

"Could you call Kemi for me please?"

Tolu got up and started to pick the bottles.

"Leave them, she will do it."

"I can as well," she used the serviette paper Kemi placed on the table to sweep the biscuit crumbs on the table into the tray. She went to the other office and soon came back with Kemi trailing.

"Kemi we're through, we can all leave now. Do you have your car around?"

Kemi moved to where the air conditioner's switch was, to turn it off. "Yes."

Tolu packed all the papers of accounts they had used together, and set them aside on Ben's table. The secretary left them and went to her office to switch off the electrical appliances. As soon as she was out of earshot, Tolu asked Ben,

"May I go now?"

"Yes, you can wait for me downstairs. I promised I'd drop you,"

"Very manly, but you may not bother. I'll find my way." She retorted, "Besides, I have to go back to the office for my bag."

Picking up his jacket, he replied firmly, "I'll take you."

Some minutes later, she was seated in his Mercedes Benz car, ready to go home. Tolu sat silent, looking out of the tinted window on her side not wanting to look Ben's way, as he maneuvered the powerful car out of the parking lot and on to the main road.

He slowed down to turn a corner, and he heard someone call his name. He looked at where the voice came from, and saw a friend he hadn't seen in a while. He pulled the car to a side.

"A.Y.O. dot. How are you?"

Ayo drew near to Ben's car. "*Ben Ben, you still dey this country? Bawo ni?*" Then he noticed Tolu in the car. "Madam good evening,"

"Good evening," Tolu answered.

"Which way are you going?"

"We are going towards Surulere."

"Let me go with you to Stadium." Ayo said.

Ben stretched his hand and opened the back door. "Come in. So where are you now?" He asked his friend as he pulled out on to the street again and drove on.

They chatted till they reached Stadium and he parked.

As Ayo got down thanking Ben, he saw Tolu's face clearly. "But Ben, I know your wife." And to Tolu he said,

"Are you not in Amman and Roche? Do you know Ifeoma?"

Tolu turned to look at him and recognized him.

"How is everything? It's nice seeing you again." They talked some more and Ayo left.

After some minutes silence, Ben murmured, laughter evident in his voice, "My wife."

"Forget he said that."

"Why didn't you deny it when he referred to you as my wife?" he asked her, glancing her way, then back at the road.

Tolu frowned at him, eyes flashing, "What did you expect me to do, tell him – *no no no, I'm not his wife, don't call me his wife?*"

"Well he left believing you're my wife,"

"It doesn't matter. He will soon realize I'm not. And most importantly, you and I know that I'm not."

"Yet," Ben added.

Tolu looked at him sharply, "Never!"

"Never say never. Have you ever heard that phrase? You are a Christian, don't you know by now that your thoughts may not be God's thoughts, and He works in various ways?"

Tolu was surprised to hear him say this. *But he is not a Christian, how come he's saying this?*

"Another thing - it's important we both get something clear. It's over between us, relationship wise, isn't it?" he looked at her again.

"Definitely." Tolu said angrily. "What kind of question is that?"

"I know what I'm talking about. I don't want us to assume anything. So it's over between us, right?"

"Right."

"Fine."

"Fine." They didn't talk again until they reached her house.

Later, as she lay in bed, she thought about the moment she was in Ben's office. She had felt some current that seemed to flow between them, or was it merely a fabrication of her mind? It must be, she said. She also remembered the slight unsteadiness of her hand as she pushed the car door open to get out, when she reached her house. Well, there was nothing to her reaction to Ben except for the fact that since she had had a relationship with him before, it was only natural to still have memories of some things and still be aware of him as a man. That was all it was, she told herself. But it was up to her to make sure she exercised self control and keep her senses.

She closed her eyes and started talking to God, baring her heart and asking Him to help her and make her strong to glorify Him in that office. She also prayed that every feeling she might have for him should leave, and Ben too should lose interest in her completely after all, he must be married. Then she slept.

The following two weeks she didn't see much of Ben, and when she did, he was so business-like towards her, that Tolu had wondered if the current she felt flowing between them had been imagined by her.

On Tuesday morning, she received a call from a customer. "I'm calling from Abuja. My name is Lahme. I called yesterday and spoke with Mr.Chucks about some goods. The agreement was for me to transfer N350,000 into the company's account, which I have done. I want him to confirm from the bank, so the goods can be sent to me by tomorrow. The company is Lameed and Sons."

"Yes Lahme. Mr.Chucks is not on seat, but I'm aware of the arrangement. I'll confirm from the bank now."

"Should I call you back in another ten minutes?" The man at the other end asked.

"Yes please."

"Who am I speaking with?"

"Tolu Pratt."

"Tolu Pratt," the man repeated the name slowly as if test driving it. "I'll call back."

"Alright."

Tolu pressed a button to cut off the line and pressed it again to turn it on. Holding the phone between her shoulder and ear she looked up the bank manager's number and dialled. She waited as the phone rang on the other end and someone picked it up.

"Hello, good morning, who is this?"

She recognized the voice. "Good morning Mr. Adeniyi, this is Tolu Pratt, Wright Investments."

"Oh madam, how are you?"

"I'm fine, and you?"

"Fine."

"Mr. Adeniyi, I want to confirm something. A customer

is supposed to have transferred some money into the account.
I want to know if it has come in."

"How much?"

Tolu was using the pencil in her hand to draw lines on a
paper as she answered, "N350,000."

"Okay, hold on, let me check."

There was silence on the other end, while Tolu waited
patiently, the phone still held to her ear.

"Hello?" The man came on line again.

"Yes Mr. Adeniyi?"

"It has come in, N350,000, from Lameed and Sons."

"That is it. Thank you very much Mr. Adeniyi."

"You're welcome. Have a nice day."

"You too, bye."

She replaced the receiver and turned to the monitor,
opening the file for the bank to update it.

Then she dialled the intercom and called the sales
department. She informed them of the payment and that they
could freight the goods to Abuja.

Just as she dropped, her phone rang. "Hello?" She said.

"It's me Lahme, is that Tolu?" he said easily, as if they
were long time friends, Tolu thought.

She told him she had confirmed the payment and
arrangements were underway to send the goods to him.

"Good. Thank you."

"You're welcome, have a nice day." Tolu replaced the
receiver.

She took the bank's file, opened it and brought out the
recent statement of account. She began to check the entries

in the statement against her own postings, ticking them off, one by one. She got to the bank's charges and stopped, with a frown she used the pencil to circle the COT charges. This is too much. She drew the calculator close and began punching.

There was a knock on her door and Lekan entered.

"Lekan good morning."

"Tolu good morning. I want to discuss an issue with you." He pulled a chair close to the table and sat down. It's about my fiancee."

It was almost twenty minutes later that he got up. "Thanks Tolu. I'll give you a call when I come back in the evening."

"Alright," Tolu stood up too, to see him off. "Make sure you discuss with her. Get her to talk by all means ..."

"Hold on, there's an insect on your dress." He moved close and brushed the insect off Tolu's shoulder.

The door opened and Ben came in. He stopped abruptly at the sight of Lekan standing close to Tolu. "I must have interrupted something."

Lekan stepped back. "No, I was just leaving."

Ben looked from Tolu to Lekan, "I thought you said you were going to see your clients,"

"So I said, but I needed to see Tolu about an issue. Have a good day." And to Tolu, "Bye." Lekan took his exit.

"Good morning, Mr. Wright." Tolu said.

"Morning." He responded flatly, without looking at Tolu. "Someone is bringing some money soon. Call me as soon as he comes. We are not paying it into bank."

"Alright, Mr. Wright."

Ben turned and left.

On Friday, in the afternoon, as Tolu made to enter the restaurant opposite Wright Ally, she heard her name and looked back.

"Hey Liz, I can't believe it's you! What are you doing around or have you left Port-Harcourt?" Tolu said, hugging her friend who was obviously glad to see her.

"I'm still in Port. It's so good to see you. You're looking cute Tolu. How are you?" Liz stepped back to appreciate Tolu's dressing.

"I'm fine, when did you come in from Port?"

Still holding Tolu's hand, Liz answered. "I flew in this morning, and decided to check my cousin Ben. I'm sure he will be surprised to see you after so many years. I'm here with him, we're having lunch together. That's him talking to his friend."

Liz pointed in a direction and Tolu's heart began to race. Liz continued excitedly, "Ben won't believe it's you," and as Tolu wanted to talk, she saw Ben walking towards them.

"Ben, see who we have here!" Liz told him, expecting him to be as surprised as she was, but instead Ben answered nonchalantly,

"She works for me."

"She does? And you didn't tell me?" Liz queried. "That's wonderful. It sure didn't take you long to get her back. So when is the wedding?"

Tolu looked embarrassed, but before she could think of something to say, she heard Ben answer Liz jokingly. "When do you want it to be? I'm sure we can arrange it."

Tolu looked at him sharply. What did he mean? She

quickly responded. "Look Liz, it's not what you think. I'm just one of his many employees, that's all."

"Look, why don't we go in instead of standing here?" Ben said dryly.

"Yes, I think we should, I'm starving. Tolu, let's go in." Liz said, pulling Tolu's hand.

"No, I wouldn't want to disturb. I guess the two of you may want to talk."

"It's alright Tolu, join us." Ben cut in, sensing she wanted to turn down the invitation. Tolu looked at him. He was just being polite she thought to herself, as she went in after Liz, with Ben behind her.

A waitress put menus and water glasses on their table. Then she dipped her right hand into her pocket and brought out a pencil, ready to take their orders.

"Are you ready to order?" She said politely with a smile.

"I want fried rice."

"Same for me." Liz said

Not sure whether to order the same thing or settle for something different, Tolu quipped in, "Same here."

The lady collected the menus. "What do you want to drink?" She glanced round them.

"Water is fine for me." Ben answered.

"If you have malt I don't mind," Liz added.

"Malt as well," Tolu said.

As she sat with them, eating, she felt so self-conscious, but Liz didn't seem to notice as she chatted on, "So when did you start to work for Ben?"

"It's almost two months now."

"And how has it been, working for him?"

Tolu cast a quick glance at Ben who was eating but obviously listening to the conversation. She wondered what to say.

"Well, it's been fine. He's been very considerate and nice. I couldn't possibly get a better boss if I tried."

Ben chuckled, but still said nothing.

Changing the subject, Tolu said, "I ran into Ngozi about two months ago, you remember her, she was in our class, dark complexioned?"

"Yes, yes, is she still in Nigeria? She seemed to be making plans to travel before we graduated." Liz asked as she sipped her drink.

Dipping fork into the chicken on her plate, Tolu said, "I guess marriage changed her plans. She is now married."

"Umm. That's great."

"When will it be your turn Liz?" Tolu smiled at Liz.

"I'm waiting for Ben to get married first," Ben looked up and Liz winked at him, "You're delaying people like me," Liz told him laughingly.

That confirms finally he is not married; That's a surprise considering his looks, and status, thought Tolu, And the fact that he was not married somehow delighted her.

"Well if you're waiting for me to get married before you do, you may have to wait for some time. I want to take my time and be sure of a lot of things before I take the plunge. I need to be sure of the girl's love, her commitment level, be sure her parents, or better still, *her mother* accepts the relationship. As they say, *once bitten, twice shy,*" Ben replied, signaling to the waiter to come.

Tolu knew that was slanted at her but she refused to rise to the bait, instead she concentrated on her food.

Wiping her mouth, Liz answered, "There's nothing wrong with wanting to be sure of things before tying the knot, but it does not have to take forever, especially if you have someone like Tolu,"

Immediately, Tolu placed her glass cup down, "Liz, please I've told you..."

Ben cleared his throat and interjected, "Liz, it's over between us. Things have changed and we'd like to keep it that way, wouldn't we Tolu?"

"My sentiments precisely," she said, her tone matching his.

"And we shouldn't forget the fact that she jilted me, as far as she's concerned, it's good riddance to bad rubbish."

Tolu winced at this remark. She looked at him. At this precise moment, she had every reason to believe he was openly attacking her. Not sure of what to say, or if she should say anything at all, she remained silent.

Liz sensed the conversation was tending to a dangerous zone so she turned the subject to herself.

"Actually I'm in a relationship. The guy attends my church in Port. We're looking at December for the wedding. When I get back to Port, we'll go to our Pastor to confirm the date of the wedding."

"Which church do you attend?" Tolu couldn't help asking.

"Restoration chapel. Pastor Mike Godspower."

"Oh! I've heard of him. So you attend his church?

Does that mean you are born again?"

"Sure. I am."

"That's nice. I am too." Tolu supplied.

"But the problem now is where the wedding will take place. My mother wants it to be in her church, here in Lagos, but I want it to be in the church I attend in Port-Harcourt, that's where I gave my life to Christ, and that's where all my friends are, that's where my fiance's friends are too."

Tolu smiled, "Thank God I don't have that problem. We attend the same church in my family, so most likely, it will take place there."

"What if your man feels otherwise and wants the wedding done in his church?"

Tolu shrugged and cocked her head to one side. "No problem. Love does not insist on having its own way, But then, his reason must be good because most of the time, it's in the bride's church."

Ben got up abruptly, and pulled back his chair. He counted out the money and gave the waiter.

"Ladies, can we go, please? I have better things to do with my time than to listen to you discussing boyfriends." His voice was laced with irritation.

"Go and marry," Liz told him teasingly. Silence was the only answer she got, as Ben had started to move. Liz and Tolu too got up.

"Thanks for the meal," Tolu said to Ben.

"My pleasure."

They went out of the restaurant and crossed the road together.

As they parted, Liz said, "I'll be coming to your office in about an hour's time."

"Alright, I'll expect you," Tolu called over her shoulder.

****

Oops! What a day. Tolu groaned aloud. Why did she have to run into them or rather run into Ben. Liz had been her friend before Tolu met Ben. Even after she broke up with Ben, they had remained friends until Liz left for Port-Harcourt.

She was happy to see Liz but didn't really like how the conversation at the restaurant went. No thanks to Ben, she thought angrily. He appeared to be holding the broken relationship against her, as if it was her fault. No wonder he had been formal and withdrawn with her.

She turned to the monitor on her table and started working. She had to get her mind off Ben somehow. She continued working for some time when there was a knock on her door and it flew open, revealing Liz.

"Oh Liz, you're around,"

"Yes," Liz closed the door and sat down. She took a book from the table.

"Ben is busy with some clients now, so I thought I should quickly check you, So how are things?"

Tolu pulled off her shoes and relaxed on her chair, "Things are fine as you can see." She said gaily, spreading her upturned hands in front of her.

"Tolu, do you have time for us to talk?"

Tolu nodded, wondering what was coming, and at the same time hoping silently the chat was not going to be about

Ben, but she wasn't to be lucky.

"I assumed you and Ben were back together again but from the exchange of words at the restaurant it appears something is wrong."

"Well, nothing is wrong, it's just that we broke up and we have come to terms with that." Tolu responded lightly, using her fingers to draw zigzags on the table.

Liz was undeterred. She looked serious.

"Are you married?"

Tolu shook her head. "No, but that's not the issue."

Raising her eyebrows, Liz prompted, "What's the issue?"

Shrugging she replied, "I mean, things are not the same again, and besides, I am a Christian."

Liz gave Tolu a long look before talking, "I don't know, but I have this feeling the two of you are meant for each other, and whatever is wrong, you can work it out. There was someone in his life at a time, but I knew they were not compatible, even though she attended his church."

The mention of the church got Tolu interested in the news. "Which church?"

"Love of God Assembly."

Tolu clasped her hands together in surprise. "Ben is born again?" She asked incredulously,

"He is, Didn't he tell you?"

Tolu shook her head and sighed.

"Actually, we haven't been talking much. He behaves as if he doesn't want me around sometimes. I don't know," she concluded, throwing her hands up in resignation.

Liz considered what she said thoughtfully, **before**

speaking, "I don't think so. When I was talking with him after you left, that was not the impression he gave me. He talked nicely of you. But let me ask you," Liz moved forward on her chair, with her two hands on the table.

"Do you still feel something for him - maybe you still care a little?"

Tolu shrugged, looked into space for several seconds, a frown creasing her forehead, "I don't know, well -em- may be I think about him a lot, I think about what could have been, you understand, but I guess that's natural. I don't know if one can call that love."

Liz moved closer to the edge of her chair, "If you still have feelings for him and he feels for you too, after all these years, and you are converted, he is also converted, and after losing contact for many years, you met again, both of you still unmarried, it may be that God is working something out between you. But you cannot know for certain until you have prayed."

"I haven't prayed about it actually because I assumed he must be a non Christian, so I've been pushing the thought out of my mind. But I need to be sure. I'm a bit confused." She paused, and then continued, "I'm just trusting God to handle the whole thing for me. If it's His will, no problem, if not, I am not desperate." She cocked her head one way and then the other.

"Since you say he's a Christian, whatever God wants to do, let Him. May be I should pray that God will talk to him too if He wants us back together. Besides, Ben may have someone already in his life. Don't you think so?" Tolu looked at Liz hoping to hear her deny it.

Liz frowned and shook her head, "I don't think so, but even if there is, there is no harm in praying. If God is involved, fine, if not, it doesn't matter. At least, you would have done the proper thing that is expected of you. And you have just said you're not desperate about him, which is very good. That factor is important. If a lady gets desperate, she becomes confused and sees it as a matter of life and death. She won't be able to listen and wait for God, and the next thing is - she plays into satan's hands and marries the wrong person. All the tell-tale signs that should warn her of the impending danger in the relationship, she ignores, until problems begin."

She gazed at Tolu earnestly, "Please pray about the matter and let's see what happens, will you? I promise to pray along with you,"

Tolu nodded wordlessly.

Liz slowly stood up, "I'd better be going. Ben will be wondering what has happened to me."

"When are you leaving for Port?" Tolu asked Liz.

"Monday morning, by first flight. Let me have your card."

Tolu took out her complementary card from a case on her table. "This is it. Thank you so much." They hugged.

"I'll call you on phone and will see you when next I come around to Lagos."

"Please do. God bless, see you." Tolu saw her off.

Well, she had certainly learnt more about Ben in just three hours than she did all the time she had been working for him, Tolu thought as she came back to her office and sank in her chair. "Oh my God!" She muttered, staring at the table, ―

lost in thought.

Discovering he was still unmarried wasn't what she had expected to hear. And how awful it must have been for him to have had another unsuccessful relationship with the girl in his church. Even though she didn't have all the facts about the relationship, she felt sure Ben was not the one at fault and she didn't think he deserved to be made unhappy. She could remember he was so kind and considerate when they were still going out together. He treated her with fairness. And it was not likely that he would have changed. If anything, his personality would be even better now that he was a Christian.

But she never imagined he might be a Christian. It did not cross her mind. And suddenly her heart felt drawn to him. She wished things were different, she wished she could talk to him, she wished she could share his joys and pains. There were many questions she would have loved to ask him. She wished he would smile at her and hold her hands.

Suddenly she came to herself and realized the direction her thoughts were taking. She hissed, muttering, "Oh God, help me and take control." Saying *take control* had become a part of her and that was how she found herself repeating it that afternoon.

Tolu dropped down heavily on to her bed getting ready to sleep. Then she picked the book that was on her bedside table to read a little. She opened a page, and her church's bulletin fell down. Picking it up, she glanced through the announcements in it, and remembered that there was to be a singles' program on Saturday 28th of August. Just a week away and she had almost forgotten. Members were expected to invite their friends along. She decided to invite four of her colleagues at work and tell them a power-packed singles program would be coming up, on 28th of August.

And then suddenly it occured to her - 27th of August was Ben's birthday! She put the book in her hand down as well as the bulletin, turned on the bed, to face up.

Ben would turn thirty years. Birthdays used to be a special time for them. They would go out, visit places, eat and drink, and then end up in his apartment most times.

Remembering made Tolu feel ashamed of herself, and she shook her head. Those were times of ignorance. There was a time they visited the amusement park, and another year they went to Mayfair hotel.

And she had always given him a gift. She had bought a _

shirt, a belt, and on his - when was it - yes, his 23rd birthday, she had given him twenty three birthday cards along with a wristwatch! The remembrance of this made her mouth to curl at the sides in a smile. *I was such a kid*, she told herself.

Yes, she sure was, but she was also sure she had loved him with all her heart, and that was why she was still a little bit shocked at the turn of events. She put the bulletin back inside the book. Should she give him a birthday gift? And if she did, what would his response be? Then she decided, one good turn deserves another. The least she could do was send a gift to him on his birthday, in appreciation of his own kindness by employing her. And what should she buy?

Tolu got up, put the book back on the table and turned off the light. With the way she was going on, she would not get any sleep at all. And only sleep could take her mind off Ben. Then she began praying.

****

The following day at the close of work, Lekan was driving past Wright Investments and saw Tolu outside who was just closing. He offered to give her a ride, which she gratefully accepted. Lekan was also a Christian, and in the car, she had started telling him of the singles program on 28th of August.

"Lekan what are you doing on Saturday? I want to invite you to a program,"

"Where?"

"It's a singles program in our church. It's starting at two in the afternoon."

Lekan was silent for a brief moment. "I can't say for

sure now if it's possible for me to come, but by tomorrow I'll let you know."

Some silence, then Lekan spoke, "We have such a fellowship in our church as well, and really, it is what we need at this time."

Tolu looked sideways at him, *"Abi o."*

"I mean these teachings on singles and relationships are very necessary, considering the attitude of some people towards marriage. For instance, can you believe this? A lady said -*please pray for a Christian husband for me before I get much older. I don't like being single, and I see many women who are not even serious Christians getting husbands* - I mean some see it as a do or die affair, as if it is when someone gets married that life truly starts. And this kind of attitude causes many people to make mistakes and fall into wrong hands."

Tolu smiled, "Well actually, there are reasons for this sort of attitude. It's like the society is built for couples. If you go to a restaurant, the chairs are set in twos, no table for one person,- that sort of thing. Such ideas have been sold to young people. And in other cases, you find some parents put pressure on their kids to get married, and give the impression that there's a problem if the kids are not. Can you believe that one of my Uncles came from abroad and screamed - *Tolu! You mean you are still in this house?* - as if I was committing a crime!"

"And that's wrong. It's not fair." Lekan commented.

"And another of my Aunts saw me the other day, and she said - *You're not married yet? What's wrong?* - It irritates me when people make such comments, as if marriage is the only normal life style," Tolu contributed.

"And the danger in such wrong attitude towards marriage is that such people place an unduly heavy responsibility and expectation on marriage, thereby setting themselves for disappointment."

"Sure, they get disillusioned and frustrated."

Suddenly, Lekan observed, looking into his side mirror, "That seems to be the big boss coming in the car behind us."

"Ben?" Tolu looked back in surprise.

"Yes. I have not seen the face of the person behind the wheels, but that is definitely his car," Lekan remarked, looking into the mirror again.

"It's him," Tolu confirmed, drawing in a ragged breath, her heart beginning to pound.

"I'm sure he will be surprised to see you in my car," her companion commented wryly, with some amusement, certainly oblivious of the change in Tolu's countenance, and the tension in the air.

Tolu looked into her own side mirror, and noticed Ben's car had come close and was about to overtake from her side of the road. She sat frozen in her seat, and within seconds, his car was beside theirs.

Ben slowed down, matching their own speed. That was when he realized it was Tolu that was in the passenger seat of Lekan's car.

Surprise was written on his face, but almost as suddenly as it came, it was gone as he wound down the car's automatic door glass.

"Good evening, Mr. Wright,"Tolu acknowledged him, turning her face to her right to look at him.

"Good evening sir," Lekan called to him from his side, smiling.

"How are you?" Ben returned the greeting. "Going home?"

"Yes." Lekan answered.

"Have a nice evening then, you two," and with the wave of the hand, he was gone, the automatic door glass going back up again .

A nice evening? That was easy for him to say, but how could she have it now? Only God knew what he would be thinking, the conclusions he would be jumping to.

Well, not that it really mattered though what he thought, but somehow she would want him to know there was nothing to her ride with Lekan.

"Somehow, I have a feeling you two knew each other before you joined Wright Ally," Lekan's words broke into her thoughts.

She glanced at him sideways, "What makes you think so?" She asked, her heart pounding. Had he heard something?

Lekan shrugged, "It's just a feeling I have, coupled with one or two comments his secretary made about you."

"Wha...t? His secretary?"

"Forget I said that." Lekan said quickly, "Anyway, there was a way he was looking at you that day we were in his office, when he asked me to take you to Wright Investments,"

Tolu raised her hand up to stop him, "He wasn't looking at me in any special way, Lekan and..."

"And, the way you called his first name now, so easily, as if you've been calling him Ben for years,"

Tolu felt afraid now, "No Lekan, there's nothing between us. And I don't appreciate your discussing me with his secretary, please." She turned and looked away uncomfortably.

"I'm sorry." Lekan said.

****

As Ben drove on ahead of them, it was obvious he was in a bad mood.

Why was she going with Lekan? Could they be dating? Frowning, he told himself that it didn't matter even if they were. He wasn't interested in becoming involved with her again. But he still felt bothered, which baffled him. Then it struck him - he was jealous! Irritated with himself, he hissed and slotted in a tape, hoping the feeling would go soon as the familiar voice of his Pastor came out of the loudspeakers of the car.

****

On Tuesday, the following day on her way home, she stopped at a bookstore, deciding to buy Ben christian books for his birthday.

After looking around for a while, she finally settled for - *Something happened, and I know* - and - *Feel His touch*- both by Redels.

At home, later in the evening in her room, she wrapped the books, and addressed the card she had bought for Ben.

On Friday, at about eleven in the morning when she was

less busy, she got up, giving herself no chance for hesitation, she put the gifts and card in a bag and headed for Wright Ally.

Tolu exchanged pleasantries with Kemi, and then knocking on his door, she went in.

He greeted her normally, but his eyes were remote - Tolu observed. She slipped into the seat opposite him and before her courage could desert her, she spoke quickly.

"I just want to wish you happy birthday."

Ben looked surprised, and stopped what he was doing.

Tolu continued, "Many happy returns of the day, long life and prosperity is your portion in Jesus name."

She placed the bag carefully on his table, "This is for you."

Ben looked at her for some seconds and smiled,

"Thanks. So you remember? This is quite unexpected. I wasn't expecting it."

Then like an afterthought, his face taking on a blank look, he said, "Wouldn't Lekan mind, or did you discuss it with him that you intended to give me this ?" Ben indicated the bag.

Tolu frowned, looking puzzled. "What has this got to do with Lekan?" she knew she had it coming.

"It's just a question. From what I saw the other day, you two are close." Ben replied, with careful indifference. "Not that it matters though. If I still cared about you, it might, but I really don't. Understand! Not anymore."

Tolu managed to control her temper. "You didn't see anything Mr. Wright and we're not close in the way you are implying. He just happened to be going my way and offered to drop me." And suddenly she felt irritated by his manners.

Who was he to be implying something or demanding for an explanation when he said in no uncertain terms at the restaurant that it was over between them?

So she snapped, "Not that it is your business though,"

Ben maintained the straight look. "It's not my business, so long as whatever you do does not affect the company in any negative way, and you keep your social engagements to after office hours."

That was it! Tolu stood up abruptly, her eyes flashing. "I only wanted to drop the gift. Bye."

So much for all the efforts she had made to make his day and give him the gift.

Her heart sank. She moved towards the door.

"Tolu!" *What have I done now? Why should I annoy her when I feel the way I do about her?*

"Come back!"

She was half way to the door. Not facing him she said, "I really should be on my way." She looked away, forcing her tears back. She must not cry, she advised herself. At least, not now, may be later in her office but not now.

Ben got up from his chair, walked over and stood beside her, taking her hand in his.

"I'm sorry. Really I am. I didn't mean to upset you. I want you to know I appreciate this gesture. I'm sorry for the things I said, and for sounding harsh."

He sounded and looked like he meant it.

Tolu glanced down at his hand that took hers. This was the first time he would touch her since they met again.

"I'm sorry," he repeated

Tolu's anger evaporated. This was the real Ben she used to know, that she fell in love with. He never felt too big nor ashamed to apologise when he had to.

"Apology accepted."

"Come back and sit down,"

Ben dropped her hand and waited for her to move. Tolu came back and sat on the chair gently, keeping her gaze on the floor.

Already she felt vulnerable. Then she looked at him, their eyes meeting, and the memory of what could have been made her eyes fill with tears. She had always found him attractive, but now he looked even more so, and matured too, in the light yellow shirt and black suit he wore with a tie.

Ben picked the bag she put on his table to check the contents. This offered her an opportunity to study him without being discovered and she decided to take a quick peek at him. Ben sat down and began to unwrap the gift.

Tolu knew she should look away, she had had her quick peek, but she didn't. Holding her breath, she scanned his face, desperately hoping he would like the books she had bought for him, as he now had them in his hands, looking at them silently.

As she watched, his mouth turned into a smile, exposing even white teeth.

Suddenly he looked up, and she found herself staring into his smiling eyes. Embarrassed to have been caught staring, she returned the smile shyly.

Ben's heart did a double flip. She was beautiful, magnetizing.

She felt like asking him if he liked it, but she couldn't find her voice, he was having such a disturbing effect on her.

He put the books down and picked the card, removed it from the envelope and read it.

He smiled again. Tolu wondered what was amusing him. She wished she could know what was going on in his mind.

Then he spoke, putting the card down, and looking at the books again. "Why did you give me these?"

Tolu shrugged. "Well, it may be because I found out about your faith,"

"From who?"

"Someone who knows you."

"I'm sure I will enjoy reading them. Thanks a lot. By the way, I had planned to give myself a treat this afternoon, would you care to join me for lunch or we could make it a dinner date?"

He knew he was breaking his resolution of not talking to her but recently it was becoming too much of a strain on him emotionally. He could not ignore her any longer. All she had to do was gaze at him from beneath those eyelashes, and his pulse rate would step up.

"No, I can't make it Ben." She objected hastily.

He burst out laughing. Tolu looked at him. " W h a t ' s funny?"

"It's you. You can't seem to be able to make up your mind on what to call me," Ben said, still laughing.

Tolu joined him, "Well, l choose Mr. Wright,"

"Well, I prefer Ben, so what will you do?"

Smiling, Tolu answered. "I'll be using both. Sometimes

I'll call Ben, at other times it's Mr. Wright."

Ben laughed again.

"Anyway, back to our discussion. I want you to join me for lunch or dinner. No strings attached."

"There couldn't be, of course. It's just that I have some other things lined up for the day," she explained unconvincingly.

"You should be able to squeeze the dinner or lunch in on your program, I believe." He wasn't going to give up.

Tolu looked at him doubtfully. She was tempted to accept, greatly tempted. But she knew she was still so vulnerable where Ben was concerned. She wasn't sure she would be able to handle him, not to talk of her own emotions. They might betray her. Could it be she still loved him?

So she tried again. "I really can't make it."

Ben sensed her hesitation and doubt, "Just to honour me on my birthday. I'll drop you at home of course, if it's a dinner."

Excitement spiraled through her, but she tried to keep it from showing in her voice. "Well, maybe in the evening,"

"It's a date then. I'll call you in the evening, when I'm ready, and I should add, I'll mind my manners." He grinned.

As she walked out of his office, she was aware of his eyes boring into her departing back.

As she entered his car later that evening, she was glad on her choice of cloth for that day, she wore a navy blue jacket on her red dress. Two of the female staff saw her and waved to her. She waved back from inside the airconditioned car.

"I can imagine what they will be thinking." Tolu commented quietly,

Ben drove out from the car park into the street. "Does that bother you?"

"A little," she confessed

"Don't let it, some things can't be helped. The two of us know it's not what they may think."

"But why is it that people jump to conclusions when they see a man and a woman?"

"Beats me," Ben smiled as he drove on.

Tolu looked at him closely, "You mean you don't know why people jump to such conclusions? Because in the morning when I came to give you the gift, you jumped to it too."

Ben laughed, "I didn't jump, I was pushed."

"You were pushed?" Tolu asked him with a raised voice, "By who?"

"You," he laughed again.

Tolu joined in, "I don't remember doing any such thing Ben."

Ben smiled, "You didn't, and I didn't really mean my comments about you and Lekan. I think I only wanted to tease you, although stranger things have happened."

"Stranger things have happened? What do you mean?"

"Forget it."

"I think you were jealous." Too late, Tolu had put her thoughts into words. Ben looked sideways at her. *Why did I say that?* She changed the subject, "Where are we going?"

"I have *Ma Byte* in mind. Have you been there before?" Ben asked as he negotiated a corner.

"No."

"You'll like it."

"I'm sure I will."

In the background, the powerful lyrics of Shirley Ceaser filled the air. Tolu relaxed in her seat and sang along quietly.

Soon they reached the place, and Ben parked in the parking lot. He opened the door for Tolu and stood back, holding it wide, and then locked it behind her. The security man opened the door as they entered. Ben looked good in his outfit and Tolu felt proud to be seen with him.

Ben chose a table by the window that overlooked the parking lot, and they settled into their chairs. Sitting together in the restaurant brought back many memories for both of them. A waiter came to take their order, and left shortly.

After the waiter had left, and they were alone, Ben asked softly, "So, have you been enjoying working at Wright Investments?"

"Yeah, yep, yep," Tolu answered, not wasting words, looking at everything around but Ben.

Ben sat back and observed her.

"How are your sisters, Bibi and Moni?"

"They're fine."

The waiter returned with their drinks.

"I realize I'm actually hungry," Ben remarked, as he inserted a straw into his glass of Chapman.

There was a moment of companionable silence and she decided to ask,

"When did you get converted?"

"About the same time as you."

"Five years ago?"

"Yeah. In October."

"Really?" Tolu looked at him in admiration. "When I learnt you are a Christian, I felt so happy for you. But why didn't you mention it the day you came to my office and you were asking me if I was a Christian?"

"It was intentional," Ben smiled, revealing his set of white teeth.

Well, he was entitled to his feelings, but now that she had started talking, she might as well continue. "I'll love to know how it happened." She asked in a friendly tone.

As Ben related his salvation experience, his eyes danced and sparkled with mirth. He told her everything about his salvation, except his reason for deciding to follow his friend to church that day. He wouldn't want her to know it was because he was heart broken and depressed after she left him. How could he reveal to her that he actually went to church because he missed her, that going to church was the choice he made between two options -to go to church or to go on the bridge and jump inside the sea? But now, he had come to realize no broken relationship was worth dying for. If he had died, Tolu might not even know about it, and she would have continued to live. The waiter served their food which was chicken shrimp gumbo soup on rice. Ben continued relating his experience as they ate. When he finished, he asked her to tell her own story.

"A friend came to my room in the hostel that particular day, in the evening," Tolu began, "and just shared the gospel with me. I felt convicted in my spirit and realized I needed to change and accept the love of Jesus. So, I gave my life to Christ. Then that night when I slept, I had a dream that really scared me, someone was dragging me away to be slaughtered.

I was crying for help and begging the man to leave me, but he didn't."

Ben concentrated as Tolu related her story. "He was much stronger than I was. We almost got to the place where he intended to kill me and suddenly there was a bright light in front of us, and someone stood there. Somehow, I knew in that dream that it was Jesus, and I cried -*Jesus save me.* Jesus stretched His hand and snatched me away from the grip of that evil man. I began to thank Him and that was when I woke up. Was I afraid? When it was morning, I rushed to the friend who had preached to me and related the dream to her. She told me the dream was clear enough."

As she spoke, Ben leaned forward and stared deeply into her eyes.

She tore her eyes from his and stared down at the table as she continued, "She said I was going in the way of destruction before, but since I had given my life to Jesus He had saved me and if I should leave Him, Satan would get me again and destroy me. She opened the Bible to John 10:10 that says the thief has come to steal, to kill and to destroy but that Jesus has come to give me abundant life and she concluded by telling me that the dream was given to me by God to encourage me to be strong. Since that day, my life has changed." Tolu smiled as she ended, "End of story."

"Hmm, that was a moving one. It could make anyone give his life to Christ."

"There's something else I'd like to know, that is, if you'd like to tell me. If you choose not to, I won't be offended, and I mean it."

"What will you like to know?"

"It's just that I'm impressed with what you have been able to achieve, within such a short period – you have Wright Ally and Wright Investments. I'd love to know how it happened."

"I started with Wright Ally. Wright Investments came up last year. It all began four years ago. I was working in a computer company at that time as a branch manager. There was this particular American man, who was one of our customers. We became quite close. He liked me, and I respected him, a lot." As Ben talked, he had a faraway look in his eyes, as he thought back to the beginning of his business career.

"Then the man said he was retiring to go back to his country. He invited me to the party his business partners organized in his honour. It was at the party he called me aside. He wanted to know what I felt about having my own company, that he could give me enough money to set up."

"What? Just like that?" Tolu's eyes popped open in amazement.

Ben nodded. "I thought he was joking. He asked for my bank account number, and introduced me to some of his partners. Still, I doubted his sincerity. Could a man go that far to help someone who is in no way related to him? Just like the Israelites asked – Can God provide manna in the wilderness? My prayer was – God let your will be done. I didn't put my mind there, I just left things open, so as not to be badly disappointed."

"Oh my God!" Tolu almost couldn't believe what she was hearing.

"You can imagine how I felt when some days later, I found he had transferred thousands of dollars into my account. I was stunned. It was unbelievable."

"Oh, I'm so happy for you!" Her eyes filled with tears, in awe of what God did. "Do you still get in touch with the man?"

Ben smiled. "Of course. I see him from time to time, since I travel often. And he's very impressed with what I've been able to do, highly impressed."

Tolu's eyes sparkled, she was filled with admiration for him. "I'm impressed too." She was rewarded with his familiar grin.

After their meal they had lemon teacake as dessert. When they finished, Ben paid the bill and they left.

On their way to her house, Tolu invited Ben to the singles' fellowship.

"Tomorrow?" He asked as he was driving." I'm busy tomorrow. I have a meeting with some people. When are you likely to have another? I'd like to attend with you." The way he said it made her feel special and happy.

"Tomorrow's program is a special one, but we have the fellowship every Tuesday, can you make the next Tuesday?" Tolu asked Ben.

" Why not? Remind me on Monday. When does it start?"

" Six in the evening,"

" No problem. I should be able to make it."

As she was getting down from his car, she reminded him, "Don't forget the Tuesday's program, Ben."

"I'll be there, don't worry." He said in his husky voice which had never failed to excite her. "And thanks for everything, you've really made my day, I never thought I would have such a bashful birthday. God bless you."

SEVEN

The following Tuesday, Tolu and Ben left together for the singles fellowship. The message that was preached was - *how to prevent crises from developing in your marriage.*

Tolu sat beside Ben. This filled her with emotions and she soon found herself thinking about a lot of things. She didn't realize this until she suddenly heard the minister say - *crises don't just happen, they are caused!*

This made sense to her and she concentrated on the message. She was impressed to see Ben dip a hand into his pocket and brought out his jotter and pen to write the Bible verses and points made by the minister. She too had her book and pen and was jotting down.

At the end of the program, as they walked out of the church towards the car, Tolu stopped to greet some of her friends.

"Is that him?" One of the ladies asked aloud.

Embarrassed, Tolu cast an anxious glance at Ben, who stood patiently some feet away, wishing he didn't hear. He wasn't looking at their direction.

Tolu breathed a sigh of relief. "No, he is just a friend."

She left them to join Ben and they entered the car.

"Your friends seem to think I'm your man." *So he heard after all.*

"Mere girls gist. Don't mind them." Ben smiled.

"Did you enjoy the program?"

"Yeah it was okay. I'm glad I came - with you."

Tolu was speechless. She had not expected him to admit that, with the way things stood between them. She was glad he came with her too.

Silence. Tolu was busy with her thoughts, while Ben was struggling with his promise to keep his distance from her. He found he wanted to be with her more and more, but could they come together again? Would that not be a sin?

To calm himself, he slotted in a tape by Don Moen and started singing along. It was a song known by Tolu and she joined in.

The moment she began to sing treble, Ben switched from treble to tenor. This was how it used to be, Ben singing tenor while she sang treble. Her mind went back to the past. She could recollect a particular time when they had done a duet together - *Endless love by Diana Ross and Lionel·Ritchie* at a friend's party. There had been so much whistling and cheering when they ended.

As if reading her mind, he said with half smile, "You remember, hmm?"

She returned the smile, "How can I forget?"

"I've not forgotten too. Sometimes I think of the way we were. Do you have my photographs still?"

She looked at him before saying quietly, "No."

"No? You destroyed them?"

"Yes."

"Why?"

"No particular reason. I thought I didn't have to keep them."

She sensed a change in his mood. He breathed a mirthless laugh, "That's the irony of life. I've kept everyone of yours. But then didn't you say -*good riddance*?"

"Don't bring that in again. What I meant is ..."

"Forget it. Let's not end the day on a bad note. We've got to your house." He brought the car to a halt in front of her house.

She got down and spoke through tight lips, "Thanks for honouring my invitation."

Ben smiled, "The pleasure is mine. My regards to your family." He reached across to pull the passenger door shut. "See you tomorrow."

Later in the night Tolu stretched out on the bed and began to pray. "Why did the day have to end like that? Lord, it's like I still love Ben. But I don't know if it can be called love. And I don't know if the feelings are shared by him, what I know is, you have a reason for bringing us together. Help me to hear You, and give me Your wisdom. I don't want to go out of Your will. If it is not him, let this feeling I have for him leave, and cause the right person to come, in Jesus' name."

****

Ben sat on the sofa in his house, his legs sprawled out before him. He stared at the book he was holding –

absent -mindedly. Voices came from the television set. He struggled to read the book, but his mind kept wandering to thoughts of Tolu, he hadn't seen her since the singles' fellowship day, which was over a week. He wondered what she was doing. He tried to get her out of his mind and concentrate on the book, but to no avail.

He would love to see her. Probably he should phone. He had copied her home phone number from her C.V. What would he tell her? He asked himself. Probably he should tell her he needed to buy a lace material as gift to Liz, and he needed a female opinion on the choice of material. Liz was her friend, she wouldn't object. He decided to give it a shot.

****

A half mile away, a grey telephone rang.

Bibi picked it. "Hello?"

"Hello, this is Ben."

Bibi used her hand to beckon to Tolu, "Oh, good afternoon, hold on, she's coming."

Covering the mouth piece with a hand she mouthed, "Ben !"

Tolu came over, "Hello Ben." Her voice was cool.

"How are you?" He said in a low voice.

"I'm fine."

"What are you doing today?"

Tolu was clearly taken aback by his question . What was up? "Well, I have some things lined up. Any problem?"

Ben cleared his throat. "I need to get a lace material for Liz, your friend, in preparation for her engagement. But I need a female's opinion, in order to get a good one. And you know these market women, they're ready to rip one off. Can you go with me?"

She smiled as she listened, happy that he thought of her to go with him. But she needed to tread softly, where would going out with him lead? He hadn't said any thing in the way of a relationship, neither had he shown that he was still attracted to her. She must be careful.

"I'm going to be busy today, I'm afraid. It won't be possible for me to accompany you."

"I knew you might say that, but then I also know, as they say - one good turn deserves another. I honoured your invitation on Tuesday, the least you could do for me is to help me out now."

She wouldn't make it so easy for him. "That's not being fair Ben. You can't say I must jump to be at your beck and call just because you attended a program I invited you to. The program was for your benefit. I'm not part of the bargain." That should put him in his place.

Ben hung up.

Her brusque manner annoyed him. So much for wanting to hear her voice. Well he had heard it, no doubt. He knew certain ladies who would be thrilled and feel honoured to go out with him, and they were Christians as well. It was just that he wasn't interested in them.

****

Tolu stared at the telephone receiver in her hand. She hadn't expected that. She only wanted to play hard to get a little. She quickly put it down before others noticed what had happened.

The phone rang again almost immediately. She picked it, expecting the caller to be Ben but it was for her mother.

"Mum, it's for you." Tolu moved away.

Mrs. Pratt picked it and stayed on the phone for twenty minutes before replacing it. As she got up, the telephone shrilled again. "It's like today is for calls. Bibi pick it." Mrs. Pratt said.

"Hello?"

"Hello, is it Tolu?"

Bibi recognized the voice. "No, but she's right here. Tolu?"

It must be Ben, by the look Bibi gave her. "Hello?"

"I've been trying the line for long, was someone using it?"

"Yes. Ben I'm..."

"Tolu look ..."

They both started talking at the same time, then stopped at once.

Ben started again, "Tolu, I want to apologize for what I did. It was wrong for me to hang up on you. I'm sorry."

"I should apologize too for the way I spoke. It wasn't exactly the right thing to say."

"No problem."

Silence at both ends.

"Do you have to buy the fabric today?"

"That was my plan." He waited, was she about to change her mind?

"Can't you get anybody else to go with you ?"

"I would prefer you." Then he added, "especially since you're Liz's friend. You'll know the right colour and material to buy."

Pleasure flooded her heart. "How do we meet?"

"I'll come and pick you. In your house?"

"Yes."

"Should I come right away?"

"Yes, I'll be ready."

"Expect me in another thirty minutes."

As he dropped, he thought of what it was about her that wouldn't let him go.

Tolu moved away from the phone. "I have to go out." She said to no one in particular.

Her mother looked at her. "With Ben?"

"Yes, something has cropped up and he needs my assistance."

Her mother raised her eyebrows expecting her to elaborate. She didn't. "I want to get dressed. Excuse me."

About an hour later she was sitting in his car, on their way out.

"You look terrific!" He commented, as he looked her over. His eyes also carried the message as clearly as his words did.

"This is for you." He handed to her a small bag. "Accept it as my peace offering."

"Thank you."

As Ben drove towards Balogun market, they talked about themselves, their friends and their faith. Ben parked when they reached the market and they got down. They entered some shops, pricing different lace materials and eventually decided on a lemon coloured lace which Ben paid for.

"Let's find a place to have lunch."

Tolu shook her head. "I'm fasting."

Ben understood. "That's okay, let's go."

In the car Ben impulsively reached out and took her hand. "Thanks for coming with me. Can I see you tomorrow?" He squeezed her hand.

Tolu gently withdrew her hand. They shouldn't be seeing, more so, as she did not know where she stood with him. "Ben, I can't see you tomorrow, and I want you to stop taking my hand, there is nothing between us."

Ben frowned at her rebuff. "Why? Because of Lekan?" His face did not ask for forgiveness.

Tolu looked at him incredulously, "Lekan?" She snorted a laugh.

He held her gaze, expecting her to deny it. She didn't. She looked out the window.

Ben started the car and pulled out to the main road, his face expressionless. How could she so easily turn him away? Did she dislike him or was there someone else in her life that was making her to blow hot and cold? He thought he was getting somewhere with her.

They didn't speak to each other as Ben sped on. The traffic was very light.

When Tolu could no longer bear the strained silence, she said, "I'm sorry."

"That's the second time you'll be apologising today.

I would suggest you try thinking before speaking," he said angrily, "it will do you a world of good."

That annoyed her. "And you should try thinking before acting as well." She pressed her lips together and looked away.

They didn't speak again till they reached her house. She opened the door and got out, taking only her bag.

"What about this?' He pointed at the small cellophane bag containing the bottle of perfume.

"I don't need it." She closed the door and moved away.

In a flash, Ben had got down and came to her. "Don't be childish. Take it."

He took her hand. That annoyed her further. "Please go." She ground out. She turned and walked away but not before Ben had seen her watery eyes.

"Tolu?" he called out, but she didn't turn back. He entered his car and left.

****

"You can go in to see Pastor now, Brother Ben." The personal assistant of the Pastor of Love of God Assembly which Ben attended said.

"Thanks." Ben entered the Pastor's office. He had been waiting for the past thirty minutes just to see the Pastor. Some other people came for counselling before him, so he knew he had to wait for his turn. He had been thinking of going to discuss with his Pastor, and he finally made up his mind in the morning. He realized he needed to talk to someone and have some good advice.

He didn't seem to know what to think anymore, since

the day he set eyes on Tolu again, about three months ago.
He had thought he had forgotten the past only to realize it was
still fresh in his memory.   There were particular questions that
had been bugging him - two people who used to go out
together, after the conversion of the two of them, can they
marry if they still love each other? Should he forget about
Tolu and the feelings he seemed to still have for her? How
could he be sure of what God's will was? And what about
her mother, would she not pose a problem to the relationship
once again, assuming they got together? So many questions,
and that was why he had come to see the Pastor.

"Good afternoon Pastor."

"Good afternoon Brother Ben. How are you? Please sit
down."

"Thanks."

"I'm sure your business is doing fine." The Pastor said.
He was a young man in his thirties, married with two kids.

"Yes Pastor. Thank you very much."

The Pastor sat back in his chair and folded his hands,
looking at Ben. "So, what's the matter?"

Ben shifted on his chair and smiled. "I've come to you
for advice. There's a girl I used to go out with many years
ago, but we broke up later. Now I've met her again, and
discovered that she is now a Christian, as well, in fact she's
working for me now. The issue is that I find I still love her
somehow but I don't know if she feels the same. Can we
marry in spite of our past and all we did together when we
were in the world? Do you understand what I'm trying to say
Pastor?"

The Pastor smiled and nodded.

"I want to be sure of God's will. How can I know whether or not she's the right lady for me?" Ben stopped, waiting for the Pastor to say something.

The Pastor moved forward on his chair, his elbows on the table, and speaking intently said, "Let me tackle your questions one after the other. Firstly, your past is past. Once you are converted, it becomes your past that should not be allowed to affect your future. What you two did together in the past is no longer relevant because you are now Christians. Jesus makes the difference."

He cleared his throat before continuing, "If she were still an unbeliever, then you would have to break away from her in obedience to the word of God, but since she is a Christian, that makes her a sister in the Lord, just like any other lady in church. Now, if you think you still love her, then you should pray. Ask God to talk to you both, and then you need to call her and find out what she feels. But before anything, be sure she is truly born again. A true child of God who loves the Lord. This is very important!" Ben nodded in agreement.

"Concerning how to know the will of God, the first day you pray, you may not hear anything. You may not even hear anything for one week, but if you have prayed, and you apply all the teachings of the singles fellowship, for instance, we've talked on factors to consider when choosing a life partner, what to look for in a Christian lady, how to court - if you apply these teachings, and you have prayed, God will order your steps. Little by little, day after day, you will know what He wants for you. I must repeat though, you have to observe the girl and her ways. Is she standing in the Lord? Regenerated? That is what God will use to reveal direction. Do you understand?"

Ben nodded, "Yes, Pastor, I understand. There's one more question. That time we were together, it was her mother that broke us up. She didn't really like me. What if her feelings towards me have not changed?" Ben questioned.

"That is why I said you have to also discuss with the lady in question. If she feels the same way about you and the two of you think her mother may be a problem, just pray and agree, God will handle her for you. But you shouldn't run away because of any problem. You can always pray."

Ben heaved a deep sigh.

"Thank you very much Pastor. You have really been of tremendous help. I feel relieved."

Ben put his hand in the inner pocket of his jacket and brought out a small parcel.

"This is for you and your wife Pastor."

The parcel exchanged hands.

"Brother Ben, God bless you." The Pastor took Ben's right hand in his own right hand.

"Let me pray for you. The Lord will continue to bless you and keep you. His face will continue to shine upon you and He will be gracious to you. You will remain in the realm of having more than enough, in the name of Jesus."

Ben kept repeating Amen until the Pastor finished praying. The Pastor began to unwrap the small Parcel. "Let me open it in your presence."

He unwrapped it and found two gold wrist watches

staring at him.

"Halleluyah, God bless you Brother Ben."

"Amen, Pastor thank you very much sir, and have a nice day," The Pastor shook Ben's hand and he left.

He felt much better, Ben thought as he was driving back to his house. He would call Tolu and have a chat with her, get to know her better.

*****

The following day in the office, Nike breezed into Tolu's office. "Tolu, I have good news for you,"

Tolu, looked up, at her, "How are you Nike? I thought you've started your leave."

"I have, I've come to see you."

"What's the good news? I can see you're excited about it."

"I am. You won't believe this." Nike sat down. "That last time I saw you, when I got home, I thought about the discussion we had, and I gave my life to Christ."

Tolu's eyes widened in surprise, "Amen!"

Nike continued excitedly. "I was so happy. But I wasn't sure of what to expect from Josiah, but it turned out that God had been speaking to him as well. We agreed to attend a gospel church, not too far from my house. When the altar call was made, guess what happened?"

Tolu's eyes widened further, "He gave his life?
"Oh, thank you Jesus, You're wonderful." Tolu shook her head, in wonder, clearly surprised.

"Which church did you attend?" Just as Tolu spoke, her

telephone rang.

"Hold on, let me take this call, Hello?"

"Tolu, it's me. If you're not too busy, could you come over?"

She didn't need to ask who it was, she would recognize the voice even if she was sleeping.

"Right away?"

"Yes, Because I'll be going out soon. I'll send my driver to pick you. Is it alright with you?"

"It's okay, I'll expect him." Tolu replied.

"Who was that?" Nike asked her as she dropped the phone.

"Ben - I mean Mr. Wright."

Nike gave her a curious look, "Are you going out now?"

"No - I mean yes. He wants to see me. He's sending his driver to bring me"

"Ebano!" Nike laughed, *"Tolu, Tolu, I talk am!"*

"You no talk anything, I beg.

Nike hesitated a little, "Really Tolu, there are talks about you and Ben flying around."

Tolu sat bolt upright, "What have you heard?" she encouraged her.

"Well, it's like people have seen you together a number of times, seen you in his car, although it's none of their business, but you know," she hesitated again.

Tolu smiled, "I understand what you're saying,"

Nike raised an eyebrow, "Or is there something happening to my friend?"

Tolu smiled again, "Well, the truth is this, we knew each

other before I came here,"

Nike was all ears now, "Ordinary friends?"

"We went out together for some time but then broke up. We have not come back together again, so there's nothing happening, as far as l know. End of story." She threw her hands up in the air.

Nike frowned, "Really? But he's not yet married,"

"The feeling must be shared, and God must give the go ahead. It's not always wise to step in through a door just because it is open, it might be a trap. The fact that he's not married does not mean we should just pick up from where we stopped."

Nike thought for a while, "How serious was it then?"

"Very serious."

"What caused the separation?"

"It's a long story."

"Make it short" Nike advised.

"I'll tell you another time. Let's drop it for now." Tolu dismissed with a wave of her hand. "I'll come for your engagement on Friday when l close."

"Thanks. And on Saturday for the wedding, won't you?"

"Sure, how can I miss it?"

There was a knock, and Ben's driver stepped in.

"Oh you're around, I'll meet you outside now," Tolu told the driver,

Nike got up, "Till Friday?"

"Yes. My regards to Josiah."

When Tolu got to Wright Ally, she knocked on Ben's door.

"Come in."

Tolu looked at her wristwatch, it was eleven thirty.

"Good morning, Tolu, how are you?" Ben put down his pen.

"Fine thank you, " she replied as she took her seat. She looked at him expecting to hear why he had sent for her but instead of talking, he just kept staring at her, using his pen to tap the table. This made her flush slightly.

"You called me."

"Yes. We need to talk."

She looked at him, wondering what was coming next.

"We need to talk." Ben repeated.

"What about?" Tolu asked, her heart beating rapidly. She looked at him and felt trapped by his eyes.

For a moment he said nothing, "What are you doing after closing, we could talk over dinner."

Dinner? She had thought they were going to talk right away, there in his office.

She frantically thought of something to say, but no word came, so she shook her head instead.

Ben shook his head too, "No, this is important. You don't even know what I want to discuss, do you? And I promise not to take too much of your time." He said in a pleading manner.

"I don't know," Tolu expressed her doubt, looking away from him.

Ben considered her for few seconds before replying.

"Do you have to say - no - everytime I ask you for a favour? Do you hate me so much?"

Tolu was shocked, "Ben, how could you say that, you know that's not true," she spoke in a whispering voice.

"Alright, let's not argue over that. It won't take long, and I'll drop you, of course." He told her persuasively.

"I don't think what I'm wearing is suitable for dinner." She looked down at her dress.

Ben too looked at her. "You look okay to me, but if you'd rather get home first to change, it's alright by me. We can leave together, I'll take you home first to change."

"No no, I'll find my way home. You can pick me at home," she told him quickly.

"Will you be ready by seven thirty?"

"Yes,"

"I'll see you later then,"

When she got home in the evening, she rushed to her room and searched her wardrobe frantically, looking for something suitable to wear. She finally settled for a striped yellow and white shirt and black slacks, which she brought out and laid on her bed, before dashing to the bathroom for a quick shower.

Five minutes later, she came out and started to wear her clothes. Then she brushed her hair and put on her neck chain, matching large earrings and shoes. She regarded her reflection in the mirror and felt pleased with what she saw. She sprayed on perfume, and picked her bag.

Tolu looked at her watch. Good, she still had thirty minutes before he was due to come. She went downstairs and found her mother and sister Moni talking in the sitting room.

When she came in they looked up, and were surprised to see her dressed up to go out, "Are you going out?" her mother asked.

Tolu came closer to her mother, "Yes, I'm having dinner with Ben."

"Ben?" Mrs. Pratt queried in surprise.

Tolu flung herself down on a chair before replying, "Yes. He's coming to pick me."

Moni burst into laughter. "I knew it. I knew it was only a matter of time before you started going out with him again."

Tolu had expected such a reaction, so she calmly said, "No, it's not like that, it's not even a date. It's more of a meeting,"

"There's no problem. Just be careful and try to come back on time," her mother said.

"Of course," Tolu replied casually.

Just then she heard the sound of a car outside and her heart missed a beat. It must be him. She crossed the room to look out of the window - it was him quite alright. She picked her bag, said the necessary goodbyes and dashed out before Ben could come in to look for her.

Ben was about to get out of the car. When he saw Tolu approach, he reached over and opened the door of the other side for her. As she climbed in, she could smell the perfume he wore.

Tolu realised he had changed his clothes as well. He was now wearing a snowy white shirt and black trousers with a dinner jacket. He looked very attractive.

"You're right on time," Tolu commented.

"Yes," Ben answered, giving her a scrutinizing look. He waited for Tolu to close her door before starting the car.

Ben stopped in front of a restaurant, and they got down. He picked a table for two in a corner and pulled the chair for Tolu to take a seat, then he sat down himself.

A waitress brought the menu list to them.

"I don't want anything please. Maybe coke."

Ben considered her, "Chapman for us, and meat pies."

The waiter wrote their orders down.

When the waiter left, Ben asked her, "So how are you?"

"I'm fine." She wondered what he wanted to discuss. Was it to confess his love for her? Not likely. Could there be another problem? Her heart was racing.

"You're looking lovely."

"Thanks." *Let him say what's on his mind.*

"Was your mother at home when you were leaving?"

He definitely was taking his time, "Yes."

"Did you tell her you were having a date with me?"

"Umm,"

"What was her reaction?" Ben probed further,

Why all these questions? Tolu wondered. "Nothing."

The waitress served them their drinks, and left.

Ben obviously had some things on his mind. He circled the glass cup containing his drink with his hands and kept looking at Tolu.

"One would have thought you would be married by now, with one or two kids tagging along."

He waited for her answer.

Tolu cocked her head a little to the right, and smiled.

"Well, it shows how wrong people can be." She looked away.

"So why aren't you?"

"Well, maybe it's because I've not met the right man."

"Not even in your church?" he asked, feeling his way along.

"Not yet, but God is working something out."

Ben drank the Chapman, *God is working something out. Is there someone in her life already? Is she in love with a man? There's nothing to lose by asking.*

"Are you engaged?"

Tolu looked at him, wishing she knew what he was driving at. "No."

Ben finished his drink, Tolu sipped hers.

The meatpies were brought, and Ben picked one to eat.

Changing the line of conversation, he said abruptly,

"Why didn't you reply any of my letters?"

"Which letters? I didn't receive any letter,"

"After we broke up, I wrote several letters to you, and even arranged for some friends to check you up. You can't tell me you didn't receive any of my messages." There was anger in his tone as he spoke.

"I didn't receive your letters. Neither did I see your friends, although now that you mention it, I wonder why,"

"But it obviously didn't take you long to get over the relationship, from the reports I heard from my friends on campus about you and Gbenga. I wonder how many there have been since then. You were obviously glad to be relieved of me."

His mouth curved in a smile that didn't reach his eyes, as

he quoted her *"Good riddance to bad rubbish,* I didn't realize that was how you saw we."

She knew she shouldn't have made the statement that day, "Ben, you should know I didn't mean it. I made the statement in anger. I couldn't have meant it Ben," she pleaded

"Does that mean you sometimes say what you don't mean? Like all the love you professed to have had for me?"

Tolu didn't know what to make of that. But why was Ben talking about the past?

"Why are we talking about the past?" Tolu wondered.

"Because the past has something to do with the future"

"Well the past has passed, I've forgotten about it." Tolu did not want to enter into arguments with him. She was not up to it.

That didn't go down well with Ben, from the look on his face. Tolu tried again. "Ben, let's not dwell on the past, it's better forgotten, with everything that happened, believe me." She didn't want him to remind her of her mother's behaviours and the whole ugly episode.

Ben stared at her for some seconds.

"I believe you, and I also believe you never really did care for me as much as I cared for you or else you would not toss aside everything so easily."

Tolu was shocked by the harshness in his voice. How could he say that, and couldn't he sense that she still cared for him?

"Ben, you're wrong and you know it. You know I did care for you, and I..." She quickly swallowed the rest of the words.

She started to twist her hands. "When I said we should forget the past, I was referring to the treatment my mother gave you and all such ugly things that happened."

She paused a little, before continuing. "And on what your friends told you about me and Gbenga, there was nothing to it. Nothing happened, absolutely nothing. I told you I got converted soon after our separation."

She wanted him to believe her. She looked upset, fumbling with her glass cup.

Ben looked at her and softened his voice,

"Let's skip it. You're right after all. Let's leave it." He summoned the waitress. "Do you have gizzards?"

"It's finished, but we have snails, fried."

"Let's have some."

The waitress left, and until she came back about two minutes after, they didn't talk. She placed the plate of snails in front of them and left.

Ben took one of the prepared snails, but Tolu made no move.

Ben knew she was upset, and there was tension in the atmosphere. *I hope I have not messed up things with the way I started the conversation.* He tried to lighten it up, "My main reason for inviting you out is for us to talk, get to know each other better."

Then giving Tolu a straight look, he added, "I want to know what is happening to you,"

Tolu remained silent. She hated any form of argument with him. "Tolu," Ben called her pleadingly. Silence was his answer. "I'm sorry," he added. *That's better*, Tolu thought. She looked at him.

"Ben, it's like you still blame me for our separation, - you're still hurt, holding grudges?" She didn't want him to be her enemy.

"Not really, I only wanted to get some things clear, but like you said, it's not relevant, so let's leave it, and to answer your question, I don't blame you anymore." He smiled to add meaning to his words.

Tolu caught sight of humour in his eyes. Then she smiled, and their eyes seemed bound with the tie of their past relationship.

Ben pointed a finger in the direction of the plate of snails, and Tolu picked one.

"Let's talk about the present, why did you have to leave your former place of work? One would have thought you would like to remain there."

"Well, I actually resigned. I felt I had to."

"Why?"

"The E.D. developed some funny ideas and became difficult to handle. If I hadn't resigned, he would have fired me anyway, since I wasn't ready to play ball."

"So you chose to resign and face unemployment rather than cheapen yourself by having an affair with him?"

"I had to. It would be senseless and stupid to begin to sleep with him just to be able to keep my job. It's not worth it."

Ben smiled and looked at her appreciatively.

"I'm impressed. That's what many girls fail to realize. It's not worth it. The risks involved are too many. They could get pregnant, and STDs are there. And eventually, when the man has had his way and finds another person, the girl gets dumped, used, abused, and broken inside. It doesn't make sense."

"So you're saying you couldn't do such a thing to any of your female staff?"

'You know I wouldn't. That's not my style. If there's any lady I'm interested in, I'll come out neat and clear. It's no fun if a man has to use force or threats. But besides, I am a Christian, that makes a major difference."

There seemed to be some powerful current flowing between them now.

"Which department do you belong to in Church?" Ben asked her.

"I'm in *follow - up*, and also one of the executives of the *singles fellowship*. And you?"

"I'm head of - *faithful builders* department and I'm also an usher."

"You - an usher and HOD? How do you manage to do them?" Tolu was surprised.

"One has to create the time. It's a sacrifice."

There was some minutes silence, as Ben thought of the next question to ask her. "Is there any man in your life?"

Tolu's eyes popped open. "That's too direct."

Ben laughed. "It was intended to be. So?"

Tolu heaved a sigh. "None yet, I'm still praying," Her heart was pounding now.

"Let me give you one more prayer point. Pray about me."

Tolu was taken by surprise. Did he mean it or was he only being funny? But he ordinarily wouldn't say what he didn't mean. Could he be trying to say something?

She wasn't sure of what to say, so she uttered the first thing that came to her mind. "What about your girl?" She tried to sound casual. "I expect there will be someone somewhere."

Ben laughed. "I'm sorry to disappoint you. I'm still single and searching. Does it surprise you?"

"Well, maybe. It's not actually the answer I thought to hear."

Ben studied her face, "Are you happy or disappointed?"

Definitely happy. Tolu laughed as a cover up, so she wouldn't reveal her true feeling.

"But Liz told me there was a lady at a time."

Ben sat back on his chair. "Yes, but it didn't work out. I realised we were not so compatible."

He tried to remember the differences he and the lady had. "She talked too much for one, and sometimes too loud. Secondly it seemed she was more interested in what I could afford, so I called it off."

"Since then?" Tolu braved herself to ask.

"I've not given up on love."

The lady brought the bill to Ben, which he settled immediately, and they finished their drinks.

"Shall we?" they got up and left.

As Ben was driving towards her house to drop her they chatted.

"This weekend is Nike's wedding. Do you plan to be there?" Tolu asked him.

"The Nike in the office?"

"Yes."

"I'm traveling to lbadan tomorrow, and won't be back till Saturday evening. But may be I should give you money, to help me get a good gift for her." It was a question.

"That's alright, do you have a particular kind of gift in mind?"

"No, buy anything you feel is nice."

Ben opened the glove compartment, and brought out money.

"This is ten thousand naira." Tolu received it.

Soon they got to her house and both came down from the car. Ben came to her side and leaned on the car.

"I've actually prayed about you – about us, and there's no doubt in my heart that we're meant for each other." He took her hand. "I've not stopped loving you. I still care about you very much."

He stopped and looked into her eyes. "Do you still love me?" She nodded. "But I will have to pray."

"I will wait until you are sure. But I am sure of my feelings. You're all I want in a woman – beautiful, gentle, caring and above all, God fearing. I now know why I've not been married. A part of me was hanging out for you, waiting for you to come back. You are the bone of my bone, flesh of my flesh."

He paused for effect. "I will cherish you with all I have." He smiled into her eyes, and waited.

Tolu smiled back. "I'm so happy, Ben. I love you too. But as you said, let me pray about it. I can't give you my answer now." She said quietly.

"I will wait. Have a nice night."

"Yeah, you too, goodnight."

On Sunday, in the evening, Tolu decided to relax outside, in the compound of the house, the air being cool and inviting. She had gone to Church in the morning.

She brought a lounge chair out. Then she went in, to re-appear with a small stool and a plate containing some slices of pawpaw which she set down.

The street outside was quiet, but occasionally, cars passed by.

She had attended Nike's wedding the previous day. Waking up early, she wrapped the gifts she bought on behalf of Ben and her own gift to her, presenting them at the reception.

As Tolu sat on the chair enjoying the cool evening breeze in the compound, she felt she had reasons to believe there might be a future for her and Ben, if the conversation they had the last time they saw was anything to go by.

She shifted on the lounge chair she was sitting on, stretching her long slim legs in front of her. *Am I ready to accept him as my husband - my head? Do I want to spend the rest of my life with him? Are we compatible spiritually? Does he really love me? Is he a man who can keep to one woman?* She searched for answers from deep within her.

She began to sing and worship God, then went into prayer. "Lord, You have promised to lead me, to guide me with your eye upon me. Reveal your will to me concerning me and Ben. I want to please you, Father. If he's not the one for me, I'm willing to obey you, even though I love him, because I know your plans for me are plans of good and not of evil, to give me an expected end, to give me a future and a hope. And if he's your will for me, let things work out Lord, for us, to your glory. I put my hands in your hands, I know you will not let me fall." She began to sing the song, *"You will not let me fall..."*

The sound of the door of the house being opened made her to open her eyes and turn her head to see who was coming.

"What's happening?" Moni called out cheerfully, as she neared Tolu.

"Has the program you were watching ended?"

"Yes, but today's episode wasn't very interesting. Can I join you?"

"Oh yes, sure. Bring a chair."

"No need," Moni flung herself down on the grass beside Tolu's chair.

Moni stared at Tolu, smiling mischievously. Tolu smiled back, returning the stare fully.

"Why are you smiling?"

"How is our Ben?"

She was expecting something like that. "Our Ben is fine, I believe."

"So, what's happening?"

Tolu bent forward to pick a slice of pawpaw from the plate. She had a bite before answering. "Nothing, God is in control."

"Where does he stay?"

"Victoria Island, although I don't know where exactly." Tolu took another bite at her pawpaw.

"You've not been there?"

Tolu cast a sharp glance at her sister, "Why should I? He hasn't asked me."

"I only asked out of curiosity I guess."

There was some silence.

"We're going to Church together on Tuesday. I hope you've not forgotten?"

Moni looked away, "I've not, but I don't think I'll be able to come."

"Why not?"

Moni hesitated. "I have a date."

Tolu gave her a suspicious look. "With who? I hope it's not Fred?"

"And what is wrong with Fred?"

Tolu gave her an exasperated stare. "But Moni, we have discussed this before. This guy doesn't share your faith."

"Tolu, you're just being judgemental, you don't even know anything about Fred!"

"I don't need to know so much about him, but from what I know, he's not a Christian, is he?"

Moni tightened her lips, "He is, he goes to Church."

"Moni, how can you talk like this? You know better. Has he given his life to Jesus, as you have? Is he regenerated, blood washed?"

Tolu waited for Moni's answer.

"He may not be yet, but God can do it".

Tolu couldn't believe what she was hearing. "Moni, you know you're going against God's word. It can't work. You'll get burnt. He can't love you the way you should be loved."

"He's gentle and nice, nicer than some so-called Christians. I know he won't hurt me intentionally."

Tolu opened her mouth as if to speak but shut it again. *God please teach me what to say, give me wisdom.*

"Moni, his being nice and gentle is not the same as salvation. Come out from among them and be ye separate is what God says, and He will ..."

"Look, look, look ,Tolu, I know about all that." Moni cut in defiantly. "You definitely don't know a lot of things. This man treats me like a rare gem, as if I were an egg, he makes me feel wanted, loved. I'm happy for you that you and Ben are coming together again. I ask after him, I expect the same from you, but what do I hear? Fred is not this, he's not that." Moni looked disappointed.

Tolu breathed in, "Moni you know I love you. You're my sister. And it's love that's making me say all this. I want you to be happy. You don't need to go out with a man to know you're wanted or loved."

Tolu looked at her pleadingly, "You made commitments to Jesus, what about them? What about your promise to obey His every word?"

Moni looked sober now, "I know, I still want to obey Him - but, I don't want to lose Fred, I've been disappointed before."

Tolu put her left hand around her sister's shoulders. "All things work together for good for those who love God, who are called according to His purpose. You don't have to compromise or lower your standards. Moni, look at me now. I didn't think I would still be single at this age, but I am. And yet, I'm willing to wait if God says it's not Ben. Obedience is better than sacrifice."

"But Fred loves me, I don't want to break his heart, I don't want to hurt him. I've experienced how it feels."

"Don't worry, Moni, I understand what you mean. But some things can't be helped, and a man has to do what a man has to do. To obey God sometimes may mean sacrifice, but at the end, one will rejoice. Don't consider the pleasure of the moment, rather set your eyes on the joy of the future. Believe me Moni, everything will turn out right."

Moni sighed and got up, "Pray for me, and pray that Fred will be saved." And with that she went back inside.

Tolu felt drained of strength. *What is happening to my sister, God?*

Some thirty minutes later, Tolu got up and went inside the house. She knocked on her mother's door. "Mum, are you alone?"

"Yes, come inside."

Tolu opened the door and entered the room.

Mrs. Pratt looked up at her daughter questioningly.

Tolu sat on the edge of the bed. "I just want to discuss an issue with you." She licked her lips.

Her mother put the Bible she was reading down and

removed her reading glasses. "What is it?"

"Ben has sort of proposed to me."

Her mother continued to look at her, expecting her to continue. When Tolu didn't, she asked, "Sort of proposed?"

"Well he asked me to pray about us, about our coming together,"

"And have you given him your answer?"

"No."

"When was that?"

"This last week."

Her mother smiled, "So, go to God in prayer." She encouraged.

Tolu cocked her head to a side. "I've actually been praying about it for some time."

Her mother smiled again and shifted her position on the bed. "I've been praying on my own as well concerning it, since the day I came to your office and saw him. It just dropped in my spirit that he might be the right man for you. Something clicked in my spirit."

Tolu stared at her Mum. "Really? So what do you think?"

"Do you love him?"

"Yes."

"Does he feel the same way about you?"

"I believe so."

Her mother thought of another question. "From what you've been telling me about him, can we conclude that he is a committed child of God?"

Tolu nodded. "I have reasons to believe that."

"Since you've been praying, what do you think God is

saying?"

Tolu twisted a side of her mouth in a smile. "Well," she drawled, "I feel he is the one, but I want your opinion on it as well."

Her mother smiled and took her hand. "I feel so too. I believe he is right for you. I decided not to say anything about what I received concerning the two of you. I wanted God to work it out without man's intervention."

"So, should I give him my answer?"

"I feel so, and if you're sure you are ready to spend the rest of your life with him, then you can."

The following day, on Monday, Tolu took extra care with her dressing, choosing a flowery flowing gown to wear, She always looked fabulous in it. As she slipped it on, she told herself her wanting to look beautiful had nothing to do with Ben, but deep down in her heart, she knew that was just half the truth. A smile shaped her lips as she thought of him.

She went to the office and set to work immediately, checking the sales and bank books. She was so engrossed in the work, that the opening of the door startled her. She looked up and practically screamed when she saw Ben.

"How are you?" Ben asked, as he sat down.

"I'm fine, how was your trip?"

"It was successful." He handed the small paper bag in his hand to Tolu. "This is for you."

"Hey, you shouldn't have bothered. Thank you."

"My pleasure. Did you miss me at all?" He asked teasingly.

Tolu smiled and nodded. She had actually missed him.

She unwrapped the gift. It was a yellow velvet kaftan.
She held it up with her hands, in admiration.

"This is lovely, Ben. Thank you very much."

"I'm glad you like it. How was Nike's wedding?"

"Oh it was okay. I gave her your gift. I bought an electric
mixer, you should have seen it."

"How is your family? Bibi, Moni?"

Tolu frowned a little and hissed, "They're okay." Her
voice was dry.

"But?" Ben didn't miss the dryness in her voice.

"Nothing."

"There's obviously something not quite right."

"It's Moni, she's been seeing a guy who is not a Christian,
and she was kind of defending the relationship. I don't want
her to make a mistake. I don't know how to handle it." As
she spoke he listened intently, with piercing eyes that seemed
to see into the depth of her soul.

Then he spoke. "You cannot handle her, only God can.
Is she saved?"

"Yes, that's the problem. Sometimes you can't tell if she
is."

"Well, you can only advise her. And you can pray for her
salvation, and pray again and again until something happens,
and we can start right away." He took her hand, "Will you
want me to pray with you about it?"

"Yes please."

He began to pray for God's intervention in Moni's
situation, to which Tolu responded with - Amen.

"What about Bibi? What are her plans?"

"Bibi is okay."

The door opened and Mr. Chucks popped in his head.

"You have a call Mr. Wright, from Wright Ally."

"Transfer it."

The intercom on Tolu's table shrilled, "Yes who is it?" Ben asked.

After some minutes, he dropped the receiver. "Someone is waiting for me in the office, I'll come for you in the evening to drop you at home."

"I'd appreciate that."

Ben got up, "I'll see you later. Bye."

True to his word, he came at closing. Tolu heard his voice in the main office, speaking with some staff. She quickly got up and picked her bag to meet him outside. Eyes trailed them as they left.

As Ben drove the car towards her house they reminisced about the past years and friends they shared. The conversation was light, full of laughter and Tolu found herself having a great time. Ben was so easy to talk with, a good listener as well as a terrific storyteller.

Suddenly Ben's cell phone rang. "Excuse me," he told Tolu. Picking the handset, and pressing okay, "Hello, who is this?" As he spoke on phone, Tolu looked at him.

"I have to see someone please," he said to Tolu switching off the handset. "The person wants to see me this evening. Are you in a hurry to get home?"

She shook her head, "Not really. Where does the person live?"

"Gbagada. If you go with me, she won't delay me _

unnecessarily. She's like an aunt to me."

As they drove across town, Tolu observed the many shops and buildings they passed.

Ben finally stopped in front of a house. They got out of the car and walked the long sidewalk that led inside. He pressed the button next to the dark wooden door and waited. Some minutes passed before the door opened and a middle aged woman greeted them.

"Oh, you're here, Ben." She said, opening the door wide. "Good evening." She acknowledged Tolu.

"Good evening ma."

She moved aside for them to enter. "Please come in."

As they sat down, Ben placed a hand on Tolu's shoulders. "Aunty, this is Tolu, my friend. Tolu, meet Mrs. Areago."

Tolu stood up again. "It's a pleasure to meet you ma."

"It's a joy meeting you," Mrs. Areago said warmly. Then she asked Ben mischievously, "Is she an ordinary friend, or a friend indeed?"

Ben laughed while Tolu smiled. "Well, she's a very good friend of mine. Very, very good friend."

"Then she's a friend indeed." Mrs. Areago concluded with a smile. She turned to leave.

"Where are the angels?" Ben asked.

"They're inside." She went towards the end of the room and opened a door. "Dupe, Sade, Uncle Ben is here. Come and greet him."

The door opened wider, and two girls came bouncing into the sitting room.

"Dupe, Sade, how are you?"

"Good evening, Uncle." They came over.

"Good evening, Aunty."

"Good evening, how are you?" Tolu greeted them.

"Fine." They chorused.

Tolu moved, and patted the space created between her and Ben. The obviously older girl, Sade sat down, while Dupe jumped on Ben's laps.

"Make yourselves comfortable. Excuse me," their mother said and left the room.

Tolu turned to the children, "How old are you?" Four eyes turned on her and hesitantly lit up.

"I'm seven." Sade said.

"I'm five."

"She is Aunty Tolu," Ben supplied.

Dupe turned to face him. "Is she your wife?"

Ben laughed, and exchanged glances with Tolu. "Not yet."

Mrs. Areago came back carrying a tray of drinks. Tolu got up and met her midway into the room and took the tray from her. She walked back and placed it on a table where Ben was, handing him a drink.

"Tolu, I hope you don't mind, I want some minutes with Ben."

Tolu smiled, "No problem ma, Dupe and Sade will keep me company." She pulled Dupe from Ben to her laps, and began to chat with them, while Ben went to Mrs. Areago.

"Would you like me to draw pictures of you?" Tolu offered.

"Can you draw?" Dupe asked.

"Yes. A little. You'll like it. Sade, do you have drawing sheets?"

"Yes. Let me bring my drawing book. Do you need pencil?"

"Definitely."

Sade left and soon came back with pencil and drawing book.

"Dupe, stand up, and stand still." Dupe did, suppressing her laughter, as she stared at Tolu.

Tolu began drawing, giving quick glances at Dupe and back to her drawing, while Sade looked on, giggling.

She finished and detached the sheet, handing it over to Dupe. Dupe and her sister began to laugh.

"Mummy, come and see," Dupe ran to Mrs. Areago. "Aunty drew a picture of me."

Ben and Mrs. Areago looked at it.

"Hey, this is nice. Did you say thank you to her?"

"Yes."

"Sade, your turn." Tolu told the other girl, and began doing a second sketch.

The girls compared the drawings when Tolu finished, laughing and chatting.

Ben and Mrs. Areago came over. "Mum, see mine." Sade gave the sheet to her mother. "Isn't it nice?"

"Very nice. Tolu, thank you."

"We'll paste them on the wall in our room." Sade said.

Ben looked at Tolu with admiration, "So you still draw."

"Yes."

He checked his watch. "Phew, it's eight already." He

and Tolu got up, "We have to leave. I'll call you tomorrow. My regards to your husband."

"Okay, I'll expect your call. Tolu nice meeting you again. And thanks for doing those sketches of my daughters."

"I'm glad they love them."

"Bye."

They soon got to her house and Ben went in with her to greet her parents. They came out a short while later. As they walked towards his car, he reached for her hand, and shyly, she slipped her hand in his.

****

Tolu's office door suddenly opened the following day and Ben came in, with Bibi behind him. Clearly surprised, she smiled, opening her mouth to greet them, but a closer look at them told her something was wrong. She looked from Bibi to Ben and then back to Bibi who looked worried.

"Bibi, what's the problem?" She asked, getting up.

Ben put his arm round her shoulders, "Moni had an accident..."

"Accident? How come? Where?"

Bibi moved close to her, "I'm not sure, I've not seen her. But her friend who phoned me said she had gone to see Fred. It was when she left there that she had the accident."

Tolu looked at Ben questioningly, and held his hand with trembling hands, "Is - is she dead?"

Ben managed a smile and gave her shoulder a reassuring squeeze, "No, I don't think so. Let's go and check her."

"She's in Kingston hospital. That's where they rushed her to." Bibi added.

Tolu picked her bag and looked around her table. "I'm set, let's go. What about Mum and Dad? Have they heard?" she asked as they left her office.

"I've phoned Mum." Bibi answered.

As Ben drove towards the hospital, he began to pray in tongues. Twice he took her hand and squeezed it, assuring her everything would be alright.

When they reached the hospital, they raced upstairs to the room Moni was in.

Mrs. Pratt was already there, sitting on a chair beside Moni's bed with Esther, Moni's friend. The three of them went straight to Mrs. Pratt.

"Mummy how is she?" Tolu asked, observing Moni's still form. Her head was wrapped to hold in place gauzy pad over a spot.

Mrs. Pratt breathed in heavily, "She's been sedated. She's been sleeping since I came in. She has not talked,"

Tolu looked at Esther. "How did it happen?"

Esther straightened up. "I went with her to Fred's house this morning. When we got there, we found him with another lady. That was how Moni just fled out. I called her, but she didn't stop. She wanted to cross the road, that was when she was hit by a motorbike."

"What did the doctor say, Mummy?" Bibi asked.

"It's the injury to her head. He said she will have to stay for about two days for observation, and of course she has bruises, here and there. But I wish she will wake up so that I can be sure she's alright, And I warned her about that man. I warned her. See the problem she has caused now."

Tears ran down Mrs. Pratt's face. Seeing tears on their Mother's face made Tolu and Bibi to start crying as well.

Ben drew close to them and placed a hand round each of their shoulders. "There's no need to cry. Crying won't help her now, what you should do is pray," Ben said in a kind, but firm voice. Then he produced his handkerchief and pushed it into Tolu's hand. "Tolu," he called her in a whisper. "Don't worry," he added anxiously, his face searching Tolu's eyes.

She used the handkerchief to clean her face, then moved closer to Moni. She placed her hand on Moni's head and prayed aloud, while the others said Amen.

"Moni, open your eyes and talk to me." Tolu heard her mother say and she pulled away from Ben to her mother. Ben followed her.

"She will soon wake up and talk to you." Ben said as if he knew for certain.

A nurse came in and checked Moni.

"*Sisi mi*, how is she please? When is she going to wake up?" Mrs. Pratt asked.

The nurse smiled and answered, "Mama, don't worry, she'll be okay. She will wake up soon. The effect of the sedative will soon wear off." And with that she left.

Just then, Moni stirred and opened her eyes. All of them came near her anxiously, while Mrs. Pratt was calling her name repeatedly. She looked at them dully, as she tried to gain consciousness. At last, she recognized their faces.

"Mummy," she croaked.

Mrs. Pratt held her hand, "Moni, can you talk?"

She nodded. "Where am I?"

"You're in the hospital."

She looked round the room. "What happened to me?"

"You had an accident."

She frowned, struggling to remember. "An accident? Where?"

"You went to Fred's house. It was when you left his place."

She thought for some seconds, then she remembered. She remembered pressing his bell several times before he finally opened. She remembered he looked surprised at seeing her. She remembered a female voice asking from his room - *Honey who is it?* Then she remembered her running away and Esther calling her name.

Moni looked round and rested her eyes on Esther, "Where is Fred?"

"He's not here." Esther answered.

"Does he know I'm here?"

"Yes."

Mrs. Pratt decided to cut in, "Moni, how does your head feel? Is the pain much?"

She shook her head. "Not so much, but I have a headache."

"How do you feel?" Tolu asked.

"I'll be okay."

"Would you like to eat something?"

Moni struggled to sit up. Esther and Bibi helped her and pushed pillows behind her to prop her up.

"Maybe rice."

"Will fried rice be alright? We can get it across the

road." Tolu asked her.

Moni nodded. "What time is it?"

"Forty five minutes after two." Tolu answered and picked her bag. "Let me get the food for her." She said to no one in particular, then she turned to Ben. "I'll soon be back."

Ben turned and motioned for her to lead, following her outside.

They came back about thirty minutes later with fried rice for Moni and snacks and juice for every other person.

Ben excused himself to go back to the office, promising to come back in the evening.

****

He came back at eight o clock and stayed until Tolu was ready to leave. Mrs. Pratt chose to stay overnight in the hospital with Moni.

Almost immediately she entered the car, Tolu fell into an exhausted sleep. Ben reclined her seat to make her more comfortable. She didn't wake up until the car came to a stop in front of her house.

She rubbed her eyes with her hand, "Oh my God, I didn't realize I was so tired."

Ben smiled at her, "Sleeping beauty."

"Oh indeed." Tolu got out of the car. Ben got down and came round to stand beside her.

"Will you be going to the hospital tomorrow morning?" He used his hand to brush back her hair.

She nodded. "I'll be in the office first, and go later, I guess."

"Hmm." He nodded, shoving his hands into the pockets of his trousers. "I'll call you in the morning then."

"You've been wonderful, Ben, I want you to know I appreciate it." She said, smiling into his eyes.

"Anything for you. I'll see you tomorrow."

"Yeah, thanks." She waved at him and moved away from the car. Ben entered and backed the car out smoothly, driving away into the night.

The following day, Ben sent his driver to take Tolu to the hospital. When he closed from the office he went there himself. The room Moni was in was filled with family and friends. Ben moved into the room and searched for familiar faces. Tolu came to him and greeted him warmly. Ben went over to greet her parents,

"Moni how are you feeling?" Ben asked Moni, smiling down at her on the bed.

"Much better, Uncle Ben, Thanks."

After some minutes Mrs. Pratt called Ben outside, to discuss with him. Ben and Tolu looked at each other before Ben drew himself to full length and followed Mrs. Pratt outside. They stood at the balcony.

"Tolu told me how nice you have been to her."

"It's my pleasure ma."

"She also told me you are considering marriage." Ben smiled, saying nothing.

Mrs. Pratt paused a while, thinking of how to start what she had to say, "Actually the reason I wanted to see you is to explain why I did those things I did when you and Tolu were together."

Ben was surprised Mrs. Pratt wanted to explain her actions. "You don't need to explain why you did what you did ma. It's all in the past."

Mrs. Pratt raised a hand up to silence him. "Don't worry, let me say what I want to say. I feel I owe you an explanation. When was it, six years ago or seven?"

"Almost seven." Ben answered, shifting on his legs.

"Right. There was a time I decided to search my daughter's bag, and I found pills in it,"

"Pills?"

"Contraceptive pills." She looked at Ben meaningfully. Ben smiled.

"Actually, I sensed you two were getting very serious about the whole thing, but I didn't know how serious you were until I discovered the pills in her bag. I felt terrified. I felt I was failing in my responsibilities as a mother, if my daughter could be using pills at the age of twenty one."

She cleared her throat before continuing. "You know I wasn't born again at that time, I believed men from Ogun state don't make good husbands but I know better now." She said and smiled.

"I was confused, and needed to take some drastic steps. I would have done anything just to be sure the two of you got my message." She stopped, smiled again to calm the atmosphere.

"But thank God the two of you are now Christians. Whatever God wants, I don't intend to stand in His way." She looked at Ben, straight in the eye.

Ben smiled and cleared his throat. "I'm glad to hear that ma."

"So many times after I did those things, it occurred to me that I could have overdone them. Anyway I just thought I should clear the ground about the past, and let you know I don't hate you as a person."

"Thank you very much for all you've said. Em, all the things that happened, are all in the past," Ben was saying.

"Including the pills?" Mrs. Pratt cut in jokingly.

"Yeah, including the pills." They laughed.

"Really, we were actually kids who knew nothing. And about some things you did and said, I've thought about them over the years, and there were times I didn't appreciate them. But I'm glad to hear you say now that you don't hate me, because em," he paused, searching for the right words.

"Tolu is still a special lady in my life. I still love her and will like to marry her."

"And you have my blessing. I have reasons to believe you're right for her." Mrs. Pratt smiled.

"So, how is your business?"

"It's doing well. God has been faithful."

"What about your parents? How are they?"

"My mother is fine. I lost Dad two years ago."

Mrs. Pratt opened her eyes wide in disbelief, "Lost your Dad? What happened?"

"He had an accident on his way back from a trip."

"Oh my God. I'm so sorry. Accept my sympathy."

"Thank you ma."

"I think that will be all for now. May God's mercies and blessings continue with you in Jesus name."

Tolu sat on the bed, in Bibi's room, chatting with her as her sister put finishing touches to her dressing. She often got invited to programs to minister in songs. She had two other ladies who usually accompanied her, to back her up.

Bibi stood in front of Tolu and turned her back, "Please, pull the zip for me."

Tolu started to pull the zip. "When is the program starting?"

"Two o clock."

Tolu looked up at the clock on the wall. "It's one already, what's your arrangement with your back up singers? Are you joining them there or you're picking them up?"

Bibi moved away, combing her hair in front of the full length mirror. "We're meeting at the program, I just hope Lanre comes on time because I'd like to rehearse a little with those ladies."

Bibi faced Tolu, "How is my hair?"

Tolu glanced at her sister's hair, "It's fine, and your dress is lovely as well, before you ask me."

Bibi smiled, "Thanks. I don't know why, but I feel a bit jittery about this place I'm going. It's not my usual crowd."

"Don't worry, just be yourself. Pray and forget about the kind of people that are there. Just minister to them. See yourself as having something they need. I think your powder is a little too much."

Bibi checked her face in the mirror. She brought out a handkerchief from her bag and wiped her face. Tolu got up and stood behind Bibi and helped her to tuck in properly a straying hair.

"Is *strong arms of grace* one of the songs you will be singing?"

"Yes."

"I just love that song. It brings me close to heaven," Tolu remarked.

"That's what a good song should do."

Tolu began humming the song, Bibi brought out her shoes and started to clean them.

"I hope Lanre comes on time. I'd like to get there in good time. I hate being late and having to rush around."

The door bell rang.

"That should be him," Tolu said as Bibi wore her shoes hurriedly. They went to the parlour. Tolu flung the door open with a ready smile and came face to face with Ben.

Bibi's eagerness turned into surprise. Her mouth dropped open in surprise while Tolu stood rooted to the same spot.

"Good afternoon," Bibi greeted him.

Ben stepped inside and smiled politely at her. "Good afternoon. Going out?"

"Yes, I thought it was the person coming to pick me that arrived,"

"I'm sure he will soon be around." Ben told Bibi but his eyes were now on Tolu who was also looking at him.

"Tolu how are you?" He looked every inch handsome in the black trousers and green shirt he wore.

Tolu blinked a few times, her heart racing. "I'm fine."

The sound of another car driving into the compound met their ears and Bibi quickly walked to the window to check the new arrival. "Lanre has come, I'm off. Tolu bye." Then she looked at Ben, "Bye. I hope we'll see soon."

"Bye Bibi." Tolu responded as Bibi dashed out, closing the door behind her.

Tolu sat on the nearest three seater sofa, and Ben sat down on a chair.

"What are you doing here?"

He gave a wry smile, "Fine thank you, I'm glad to see you too."

Tolu frowned, "What? Oh!" The meaning of the reply he gave dawned on her. "I'm sorry, but why didn't you tell me you would be coming?"

Ben gave her a scrutinizing look, to determine what she felt, "Do I take that to mean I'm not welcome?"

"No no, of course not. It's just that you were the last person I expected to see. I would have thought you would mention it in the office yesterday."

"I felt like checking you. I didn't realize my visit might be resented," Ben pretended to be offended.

"No. That's not true. I just wasn't expecting you. What do I offer you?" Tolu stood up, giving him a reconciliatory smile.

"Are your parents at home?" He wanted to know.

"No they've gone out."

"Are you the only one around?"

"Yes."

Tolu clasped her hands together in front of her, "What do I offer you? We have malt, Ice cream,"

"Ice cream will do. Thanks." Ben looked around the sitting room.

"Just a minute please," Tolu said before disappearing into the kitchen.

She opened the deep freezer and brought out the plastic containing the ice cream. She took a small glass cup and filled it with ice cream. Placing the cup of ice cream on a tray, she put a spoon beside it. She cut the cake into small pieces and neatly arranged them on a plate. She placed the plate on the tray as well and carried it into the sitting room, putting it on a side stool in front of Ben.

"Thanks."

"You're welcome." Tolu replied as she sat down. She used her left hand to sweep the strands of hair in her face back, and then it occurred to her. Her hair and her dressing! She must look a sight!

"I didn't know I could have any visitor today. See my hair!" she exclaimed.

Ben looked her over, "You look okay to me. What have you been doing?"

"I washed my clothes in the morning, and I planned to probably watch some video tapes later on this afternoon,"

Ben picked a slice of cake and ate, "Wouldn't it be boring for you, being at home, alone?"

"Well -" She drawled,

"I hope you won't mind if I change your plan a little. Spend the day with me."

"With you?" She was clearly surprised and thrilled.

"What do you have in mind?" She felt flattered that he wanted to spend the day with her.

"I need to see my mother. I don't mind our going together." He was taking the ice-cream and cake.

"Go with you to your mother's place? I can't." She shook her head. "I haven't seen her in years."

Ben was looking at her amusedly.

"Why can't you? Although, if you'd rather go somewhere else, it's alright by me."

Tolu thought about it and shook her head, "I've not seen her in a long while. I can't just turn up on her doorstep like that. It will give a wrong impression."

" Wrong impression to who? If you're thinking of my mother, don't bother. She knows you're working with me, and she asks of you from time to time."

"She asks of me? But you never told me! The day I meet her, I'll let her know you never delivered her message."

Ben smiled, "Guilty as accused. Tell her when you see her today."

Tolu raised a hand up. "I haven't agreed to see her today,"

"I don't see why not. Sooner or later you will have to see her. She knows how I feel about you."

"I'm not ready to meet her today. Suggest some other place."

"What about - *God's Heritage Orphanage Home?*"

"God's Heritage Orphanage Home? Do you know anyone there?"

"Yes, it's being run by my friend's wife . You've met Boye before. There was a time you came to my office and I introduced you to a man, you remember?"

Tolu tried to remember, "He's a bit fair, he wore glasses."

"Yes that's him. I've been to the home a few times, you'll love it, and of course I'll take care of you."

"Oh I know that, Mr. Caretaker."

"Talking about caretaker, have you accepted that I become your caretaker?" He came over and perched on the arm of Tolu's chair, taking her hand. "Do you have any answer for me yet?"

Tolu's eyes beamed with the joy of love, as she answered, "I have prayed," she paused dramatically, putting Ben in suspense.

Ben asked in anticipation, "And?" He used his hand to turn her face up, so he could look into her eyes.

"And," she let the words out slowly. "My answer is... yes." She smiled at him lovingly.

Ben gathered her in his arms and kissed her on her cheeks. "I love you Tolu. You won't regret this, I can assure you."

He released her and Tolu got up. "Let me go and get dressed. I won't be long."

Tolu went upstairs to her room and closed the door. She decided to have a shower. She enjoyed the feel of the water on her body. She stepped out of the bathtub and pulled a towel from the towel rack, to mop her body and then entered her room. She threw open her wardrobe and brought out a blue coloured dress.

Gingerly, she pulled on the dress and used her hands to straighten it down. She wore her blue high heeled sandals, put on her earrings and started styling her hair in front of the mirror. She swept her hair up, leaving a few selected strands loose along the hairline. Soon she was through with that and she went to where she kept her bags and took the clutch bag she had just bought, dropped her mini purse, and a few things inside. She turned round in front of the mirror to check her appearance, before she finally went downstairs to join Ben where he was sitting down patiently, waiting for her.

Ben smiled at her appreciatively, "You're looking very beautiful. The colour of your gown brings out the beauty in your eyes."

She was glad he thought so, and she said demutely, "Thank you."

She glanced down at the cup of ice-cream and the plate, and saw that they were empty. She bent down and packed them to the kitchen, and returned to the sitting room.

"Let me drop a note for my parents and then we can go." She wrote the note and put it where her parents would see it. "I'm set if you are."

Ben stood up, "Let's go."

Tolu jammed the door lock. Ben held open the car door on passenger's side to allow Tolu to enter, and closed it gently when she did. He went round to his side and entered the car, and soon they were out of Tolu's house.

"I feel like a teenager going out on his first date. I'm

excited." Ben commented.

"I'm happy too," she relaxed on her seat.

"Do your parents still live in Ebute-meta?"

"My mother - yes." he said lightly.

Tolu shot a glance at his face, "What about your Dad?"

"He's late. Died two years ago."

"Oh no. Ben!" She exclaimed, "I didn't realize. What happened?" She looked at Ben with concern.

"He died in a motor accident, on his way back from Ife. He went with his friend. The friend survived though."

Tolu's eyes widened in shock. "Oh Ben, I'm sorry, but you didn't tell me all this while." She accused him.

"Our conversations didn't get to that."

Tolu turned on her seat and regarded him solemnly, "I really am sorry. It must have been terrible for you."

Ben tried a smile, "It was, but as you can see, I have survived. But it was a tough time."

Tolu was still looking at him, "Maybe we can check your Mum afterall."

Ben shook his head, "No way. Not today again. Not after learning about my father's death. We're to enjoy the day together, it's not to mourn. Another time you can visit her. I mentioned it to your mum that day we chatted in the hospital."

Tolu frowned, "You did? She didn't tell me."

"Obviously. Now let's talk of other things. I don't want to remember those unpleasant memories."

"Ben?"

"Yes?"

"Could you please stop for me at Landey store briefly.

I want to get some things there."

"No problem," he agreed, driving on.

Soon they reached the store and he slowed down.

"Let me find somewhere to park." He told her as he manoeuvered the car into the compound of the store.

He parked and as Tolu got out of the car, he got down too, taking the keys out of the ignition.

"I won't be a minute." Tolu told him but Ben used his hand to indicate she should preceed him.

As they neared the glass door of the store, it parted of its own accord and they entered. Tolu led the way to the area of fruits, and started to pick them into a trolley. Then she went to where crates of eggs were and put three crates in the trolley as well. Then they moved away.

"What are you doing with these?"

"For the orphanage home."

Ben was impressed. He had given a cheque to the home two weeks ago as he did every month. And today, Tolu was buying things for them as well. He knew he wasn't making a mistake in choosing to marry her. She walked to the section of cards and started checking them. Ben stopped to consider some wristwatches.

Soon Tolu came to meet him, pushing her trolley and a greeting card in her hand. "I've got all I need."

They moved to the cashier and Tolu paid. They put the groceries in the boot, and drove off.

Tolu gave the card to Ben, after addressing it.

"For me?" He removed the card from the envelope. The words he read stunned him - *"What can I say ? You are*

God's gift to me," Love from Tolu.

He looked at Tolu and back to the card, smiling. "You really mean it, honey?"

She nodded, eyes glowing, "Every word. Let me add more - you _bring out the best in me._ You have been so good and so unselfish. I just needed you to know I appreciate you." She looked at him with eyes that seemed to tell him she loved him.

He put a hand on her shoulder. "And I appreciate you too. But you know that already." His throat was suddenly dry. He felt like throwing his arms around her and kissing her.

Tolu could feel his heart beating wildly. Her heart was racing too. _God help us - I just love him._

There was contented silence for a while before Ben asked her, "Will you accept a gift from me?"

Tolu turned to look at him thoughtfully, "A gift?"

"Yes."

Tolu did a quick thinking, and tried to pick her words with carefulness. "I think it depends on what it is, and if I'm sure there is no ulterior motive behind it."

"Ulterior motive?" She saw his face stiffen and take on expression of disbelief.

"That was meant to be a joke," she quickly said.

"It must be. Why should anyone accuse me of an ulterior motive where you are concerned? If I desire to give you a gift, it's with pleasure. No hidden agenda."

He glanced sideways at her, "You've not answered my question."

"What kind of gift is it?"

"A car."

Her mouth dropped open. "A car?" She said in a whisper.

"I actually ordered it for myself, but I think I want you to have it."

"Ben, thanks for wanting me to have it, but I can't accept it."

"May I know why?"

Tolu searched for what to say, "I was thinking it might be cloth or something," she thought of more words, "You've given me cloth before..."

Ben smiled, "I gave you cloth before, now I'm giving you a car. What does it matter? A gift is a gift."

"But, I mean," she faltered, "Why should you want to give me a car?"

"If I may ask, why did you stop to buy those fruits for the Home?" Ben queried back.

Tolu looked at him consideringly, "But that's different." She argued.

Ben laughed. "And this is different as well."

He laughed again, "A man is offering you a car, and you are turning it down. But that's why I love you. Anyway, I want you to accept it."

Tolu shook her head, she thought of another excuse. "It's an expensive gift, Ben." She looked at him uneasily.

"To you it's expensive, to me, its not. Another excuse?"

Tolu was speechless.

"Look Tolu, to give you cloth or car or buy you lunch gives me pleasure. You didn't ask for it." Tolu's heart soared.

"Ben I appreciate the gesture, but I don't want to accept

such gift now, later possibly, but not now."

Ben shrugged ,"If you say so." He said as he drove into the compound of the orphanage home.

"It's likely I travel on Monday night to America for about a week. I received a fax message from one of our suppliers there, which will necessitate my travelling immediately."

"On Monday?"

"Yes. Can you worship in my church tomorrow? I'd like us to be together tomorrow as well, before I travel." He glanced at her, as he brought the car to a stop.

"I'll be there." She felt like being with him too. She had been praying about their relationship, and everything that was happening was making her more certain that Ben was the will of God for her. He seemed so different from every other man she had known. He was her best friend, and they could talk about anything. She looked forward to sharing her life with him.

****

The following Tuesday, in the afternoon, there was a knock on Tolu's door and a pregnant woman came in. She was dark skinned and obviously in her twenties.

She closed the door and moved to the chair opposite Tolu, but she didn't sit.

"Are you Tolu Pratt?" She asked in an unfriendly tone, staring at her.

Obviously thinking she was a customer, Tolu stood up to greet her.

"Yes, Good afternoon. May I help you?"

The woman gave her an icy stare, "Yes. Get out of my man's life! And stay out!"

If Tolu had been slapped, she couldn't have hurt more. What was she talking about?

"I'm not sure I understand what you said."

"You wouldn't, would you? I know your type. You feign innocence. Husband snatcher!"

"Excuse me?"

"That wouldn't be necessary. I'm not here to trade words with you or fight, at least not yet. I just want to advice you to leave him, if you know what's good for you."

Tolu's stomach turned and she suddenly felt dizzy, it couldn't be Ben, could it? "And who is the man you're talking about?"

"I'm talking about Wright!" The woman said angrily. "He promised to marry me, but since he met you, he's not seeing me again. But I'm not ready to lose what belongs to me. He is mine. You hear that? He is mine."

Then the woman lowered her voice in a pleading manner as Tolu looked on disbelievingly. "If you will not want to drop him because of me, please do it because of the little one that is involved in this." She motioned to her protruding stomach.

Waves of shock rippled through Tolu. It couldn't be true. It couldn't be. And yet, here was the well dressed woman pleading with her. She didn't look like a lunatic. She was dressed fashionably in a green linen skirt suit with jewelry and her obvious pregnancy was a proof to Tolu's startled eyes.

"I've made my investigation about you," the woman continued, "and I know where you stay with your family. If you don't drop him coolly, you will drop him by force. By the time I finish with you, you won't know what hit you."

Tolu was speechless. *This must be a dream.*

"Because I'd do anything, and I mean anything to keep him." The lady continued.

Tolu at this point thought she should say something. "Excuse me madam, I don't even know your name, I want to believe you're a Christian, why don't you..."

The woman didn't allow her to finish before hissing out, "Christianity my foot! There is a time for everything. I will not open my eyes and let what is rightfully mine slip from my hand while I am praying. And for reference, when you see him, you can tell him Rhoda Ibitoye paid you a visit. He knows he has erred, and unless he fulfils his obligation, he will have no peace! Good day." The pregnant woman stormed out.

Tolu dropped on her chair and leaned back, closing her eyes. *What have I got myself into?*

Slowly, her mind travelled back to the day she came to his office seeking his help, probably she shouldn't have come, then all this mess wouldn't have been. Ben had been nice, exceptionally nice to her, no wonder Rhoda didn't want to lose him.

From their discussions, she had assumed she knew him well enough. Obviously she didn't. She had over estimated him. Could Rhoda be the girl in his church that he dated? The woman mentioned his name, and she also knew Tolu's name, and her pregnancy was enough evidence that she had a relationship with Ben. *Oh my God! But I prayed, how can this happen to me?*

Her head began to ache as her heart pounded. Her eyes started to spin and for a moment she thought she might faint. She needed to talk to someone right away to ease the burden or she might lose her mind, with the way she was feeling, the shock was too much for her to weep.

She dialed Bibi's office telephone to inform her she was coming, then she told Mr. Chucks and others she had to go out, and with that she left.

"I can't believe this!" Bibi said in shock. "It just doesn't sound like what Ben can do."

Tolu breathed in heavily, in a perplexed manner, "That's how I felt too, but with her pregnancy, there's no doubt about it."

"You said the lady is pregnant?" Tolu nodded. With a frown Bibi asked, "And she told you Ben is responsible, she mentioned his name?"

"Yes."

There was silence, "What are you going to do now? When is Ben expected back from abroad?"

"He told me Monday."

"But Ben seems to be level headed, and a serious Christian, could he have been involved with such devilish woman, who's swearing?"

"I'm sure I didn't imagine her visit." Tolu replied.

"Even though one sees a lot of rubbish being done by some Christians but Ben didn't seem to be such a two timing, double faced lout. This is a big problem o. You have to confront him with the issue immediately he comes."

"What if he denies it? Or worse still, if he confirms it?

What will I do?" Tolu despaired.

"And you work for him. And you love him," Bibi said. It was neither a confirmation nor a question.

"But you prayed, Tolu." Bibi continued.

"I did, Bibi. And I felt sure God told me it was alright. It wasn't as if I was desperate. I wouldn't have involved myself if I hadn't felt God leading me on. And he never gave me reason to doubt his character. How will I face him at work after all this?"

Bibi looked at her watch, "It's almost time. Let's go home. We'll talk more and decide what to do." They got up and left Bibi's office.

At home Bibi made toasted bread and cold beverage drink for the two of them, and they sat at the dining table. Tolu didn't touch the bread. She sipped the drink a little and stared vacantly at the wall.

"Tolu, you have to eat something."

"With my world collapsing?"

Bibi touched Tolu's hand lightly, "You know your world is not collapsing. It's too late for the enemy to catch up with you. And as we say in church - all things work together for good, for those who love God, and who are called according to His purpose. If God allowed this to happen now, it means He is saving you from impending danger in marriage. Everything will turn out right. Een? Don't worry."

They heard the outside gate being opened and closed. Bibi got up to check. She saw her mother walking in, and she unlocked the door for her. Bibi greeted her cooly and went back to join Tolu at the dining table. Mrs. Pratt followed.

Without looking up, Tolu greeted her, "*Mummy, e kaabo*."

Unsuspecting, she greeted her daughters and began to discuss her outing. Then she stopped. "You are not talking, what's the matter?" She looked from one to the other. Bibi looked at Tolu but Tolu didn't flinch, her gaze at the wall unwavering.

Alarmed, sensing something was wrong, she sat down opposite them. "Tolu, Bibi, what is it? Where's Moni, where's your Dad? Tell me!"

Bibi smiled, "No Mum. It's not what you think, everybody is okay."

"So what is wrong - Tolu?"

When Tolu didn't speak still, Bibi spoke again, "Tolu had an uninvited visitor at work today, that's all."

"Tolu, who was it?" Her mother placed her elbows on the table and leaned forward.

Tolu bit her lip and told her mother of Rhoda Ibitoye's visit to her office and what she learned from her about Ben. As she spoke, tears coursed down her cheeks. Bibi patted her back gently.

"Impregnated the girl?" Her mother asked in disbelief. Instead of replying, Tolu tightened her lips and closed her eyes.

She was silent for a while before speaking again. "Something is wrong somewhere. I doubt if Ben can do such."

"So who put Rhoda in the family way?" Bibi asked.

"Did you say he has travelled?" Tolu nodded

"Since you began dating, did you suspect there might be another woman in his life?"

"I didn't. It didn't occur to me that someone is pregnant." Tolu said in anger.

"Any previous relationship?"

"He told me there was a lady sometime ago, but that it was over between them, that was all."

Hesitantly, her mother asked further, "Does he tell you he loves you?"

Tolu nodded, "What am I going to do now, with this other lady threatening me?"

"Don't worry about..." Her mother was saying before another thought occurred to her, "You're not pregnant are you?"

Bibi burst into laughter, "That's another thing o. Tolu?"

Tolu smiled, in the midst of her tears, "No, Mummy how can you say that? Of course not."

Mrs. Pratt breathed a sigh of relief. She reached across the table and took her daughter's hand. "Don't worry about the lady's threats. God is a very present help in time of trouble. She can't do you any harm." She paused for seconds, "When Ben comes back, you have to ask him about Rhoda, and if he confirms it, then the relationship must be broken. God has called us unto peace. You have to release him to sort himself out."

"What about the office? Should I resign or what?"

"You don't have to, unless he sacks you or something. You can continue working there, meanwhile start looking for another job. I don't know what Ben will say about Rhoda, but somehow I can feel it in my spirit that God is in control, so cheer up."

Tolu stood up, "I have headache. I'd love to have an early night."

"Let's pray then, before you turn in."

but something had stirred him. ... Tolu heard his voice... so concern:

Tolu spoke up. "Thanks... Ben, I'd love to have an early night."

"Alright, then, bye..."

CHAPTER
TEN

On Thursday, her direct line rang. Absently she picked it. "Hello, Tolu Pratt here. Who is it?"
"Hi Tolu, this is Ben."

She wasn't expecting his call, and so was unprepared as to how to handle him. She didn't speak immediately, trying to get her thoughts together.

"Tolu are you there?" Ben asked anxiously.

"Yes." She answered coolly.

"How are you, how have you been?"

His tone was pleasant and loving, not at all like someone who was double dating. How could he be so heartless, talking as if he didn't have a care in the world - Tolu thought? How could he have the nerve to live such pretence? How could he act as though he didn't know his child by Rhoda would soon come into the world? How could he do this to her.? How could she have erred so badly in her judgment of him.? Thinking he was a good man. How could she have allowed him into her life again, taking her heart with him? Her heart ached.

"Tolu, is everything all right? You're not talking." Ben's voice came on the line again.

"Yes?"

"What's been happening to you?"

"I've been busy."

"I've missed you."

Her heart lurked. *Liar.* She tried not to feel anything for him. She didn't answer.

"Tolu are you sure you're okay?"

With irritation she snapped, "I told you I'm okay, I'm just busy. In fact I'm in the middle of some work. When are you arriving precisely?" She needed to know when to expect him so she could accuse him.

He didn't seem to notice she snapped, "Monday night. That means I won't see you until Tuesday in the office. I'm looking forward to seeing you. I bought some things for you. You will love them." Ben continued good naturedly, ignoring the fact that she was not really talking.

"I'll see you on Tuesday. When I do, you'll explain what's bothering you. Even though you denied it, but you seem to forget I know you well."

Tolu didn't respond. She tried to harden her heart. She had made up her mind to break the relationship as soon he got back. She would not accept any explanation or reasons from him about Rhoda. What genuine reason would he have to give her? She must be strong, even though her heart was breaking.

"I'll see you on Tuesday. Don't forget or doubt my love and commitment to you. Bye." Ben said.

Ugh! Love and commitment indeed! He would make a good actor. Some people find it so easy to lie. It must be a gift to them, a gift she lacked. She placed the receiver back in its place.

Hearing his voice again aroused different emotions in her, and she felt the pain again. She truly loved him. How could she continue working in Wright Investments under this circumstance?

She got up and strolled out, to walk off the pain. She wished there was something she could do for her heart that was aching. She didn't feel like eating. As she walked, she thought of a song to sing, and the song she had heard in kid's praise video came to her mind, and she began to sing quietly "I cast all my cares upon you. I lay all of my burdens down at your feet, anytime, I don't know what to do, I will cast all my cares upon you."

****

Ben breezed into his office that Tuesday morning. His driver brought in only his briefcase. The gifts he had for Tolu were left in the boot of the car. He intended to go to her office later. He sat down and asked Kemi to bring in the mails that had come in when he was not around. Then he switched on the answering machine on his direct line for messages.

He had been thinking of today, throughout the week, when he was away, thinking of how he would propose to Tolu and what she would say. As soon as he had sorted out the issue of mails and messages, he would phone her first before going to Wright Investments to check her.

Kemi came in with the mails. "These are the mails that came in and this letter is from Tolu Pratt, she told me to give you."

From Tolu, what might be wrong? She did sound off hand when he called her from America.

He took the letter from Kemi with a puzzled look. He had a premonition it was not going to be good news.

He ordered Kemi to leave. He opened the letter, and he was shocked by the content. Shock was written all over his face.

No, it can't be! With a bewildered look, his mind in a turmoil, he read it through again, not believing his eyes.

He cracked his brain. What happened before. he travelled? Did they have an argument? Did he say something or do something to annoy her? She hadn't mentioned her reason for not wanting to see him again. This was not what he expected from her on his arrival. Something was wrong.

He summoned Kemi immediately. "Did Tolu mention anything to you when she was giving you this?" he held the letter up.

"No, she only said I should make sure you received it." Kemi replied wondering what was wrong.

With a far away look in his eyes he told her in a cutting tone, "Okay, you may go."

He lifted up his receiver and dialed Tolu's direct line. He waited as the number began to ring but there was no response. He cut it and dialed the general line. Mr. Chucks picked it.

"Where is Tolu?" he barked.

Recognizing his voice, Mr. Chucks quickly greeted him, "She said she would not be around today sir."

Ben's eyes narrowed. "Okay thank you." He rang off, deep in thought. What could have gone wrong between them?

Or did something happen while he was away? He tried to check in his mind what it could be, but came up with nothing. He ran his left hand through his hair roughly and breathed heavily. He must see her immediately and find out why she had written that letter.

He put the letter back in its envelope and tucked it in the inner pocket of his jacket. He made for the door, determined to get to the root of the matter. Their relationship had been broken before, and it appeared history was about to repeat itself, but he would not allow the repetition - God helping him.

****

What kind of life is this? Tolu thought bitterly. She had him but lost him. Found him again and from all indications had lost him yet once more. The one man in the world she had ever truly loved. She had tried to fight her feelings, telling herself she no longer cared but it was not working. Tears ran down her face. She moved away from the window to lay on her back in bed.

She had her legs crossed and her two hands were folded under her head. The weather was cold outside, matching her mood. Surely this was the loneliest moment of her life. She felt an agony that had no possibility of finding a release.

She had been crying since and now her eyes were puffy and red, She had never been so unhappy all her twenty seven years on the surface of the earth. She truly loved Ben, she thought. She had also realised why she hadn't been particularly interested in other men - it was because Ben was somewhere in her heart, all those years. Time had been able to mend her broken heart the other time, but she doubted if it would be able to perform the same miracle on her heart this time around. The thought of this made her laugh cynically, and she shook her head in self pity. She doubted if she would marry any other man - it wouldn't be fair to the other man when she loved Ben the way she did. Thought of having to marry another man or remaining single if Ben was truly lost to her provoked more tears.

She reached out for the handkerchief and blew her nose, before going to the toilet to ease herself. She caught a glimpse of herself in the bathroom mirror, and what she saw made her stop. The face staring back at her in the mirror looked so terrible. Her hair was disheveled. Her eyes were red and puffy, and the night - gown she still had on didn't help her looks a bit. With a resigned sigh, she entered her room, darted across to her wardrobe and brought out a pair of jeans pants and a white T. shirt, which she changed into. Then she picked up her comb and brushed her hair back from her face.

God seemed so far away and she wondered if God had forgotten her. She sat down on the bed and stared into space, humming Don Moen's song – *I will sing.*

Suddenly the doorbell rang and interrupted her thoughts. She looked up quickly. Who could it be? She wasn't expecting any visitor. The bell rang again. Tolu got up and looked at her face in the mirror. The eyes were still red, and she didn't look too presentable. She hissed and decided not to answer the door, hoping whoever it was would leave if there was no answer.

But she was not so lucky. It appeared the visitor seemed to know there was someone inside, and was determined to get through. The bell rang again and again, clearly with impatience, echoing long in the hall after the button had been pressed.

Reluctantly she got up and went to the sitting room to answer the door. She intended to dismiss whoever it was quickly, as she was in no mood for small talks or pleasantries. But still, she would need to put on a bright face, she wouldn't want the visitor to guess right away that she had been crying.

She pasted a smile on her face and asked, "Who is it?"

"Ben!" A familiar voice answered.

Her heart almost stopped beating as the smile vanished. "Ben!" She repeated, and did a quick thinking, whether or not to open the door. The need to see him was stronger than her reason to send him away, so she opened.

"Ben what do you want?" She asked bitingly.

He looked furious. "And what do you want?" He threw the question back at her.

"I want you to go away!" she said, her voice a little loud.

"Not before we discuss. I don't appreciate the letter you left for me."

Tolu stepped aside to allow him to enter. She thought of how she must look and quickly said, "I wasn't expecting to see you."

"Obviously, from the look of things." His gaze travelled over her.

Tolu closed the door and sat down. Ben did the same.

Ben sucked in his breath, "So what happened?" he asked in a rough voice.

Tolu remained silent, but she couldn't help wondering

why he was annoyed. He should have known she had discovered his secret. Why was he complicating matters as if he cared?

"What's the matter, Tolu?"

"I've already written all I have to say in the letter." She almost choked on the words as she spoke. She tried to keep the tears back, her face grim with misery.

"And you couldn't wait for me to get back to discuss with me?"

She shook her head, not looking at him. "It was better that way."

"For you or for me?" Ben demanded, looking at her closely.

Why all these questions? Why was he making it difficult for her? She had her legs crossed and her two hands were folded under her head. The weather was cold outside, matching her mood. Surely this was the loneliest moment of her life. She felt an agony that had no possibility of finding a release.

"I'm talking to you Tolu." Ben said with growing impatience. "You never told me of any problem. We were together before I travelled, and I thought we had something going for us," he hesitated and continued, "I thought you loved me."

There was silence. Lowering his voice, he asked, "Is there anything I can do to make you change your mind?"

Tolu put him right quickly, "I am not changing my mind. Nothing you can say or do will make me change my mind." She said firmly.

Ben looked at her wordlessly for some time and said, "What if I say you can't leave me?"

Tolu turned abruptly and looked at him, her eyes challenging him.

Ben rephrased his statement. "I don't want to lose you. Please, let's continue our relationship."

Tolu shook her head regretfully, "I'm afraid that's impossible. I've made up my mind. You've already lost me." She saw his body tauten. She looked at him consideringly. This was not what she expected he would be saying. He belonged to someone else. Another lady was carrying his baby, and she needed him more. He could not be hers and there was no point hanging around him.

"And what about me, don't I matter? How do you think I will feel?"

"Relieved of course."

"Relieved? Is that what you think?"

Tolu could no longer bear his show of concern. Why was he pretending there was no other woman in his life. This man had no shame. Tolu summoned up enough anger to be able to push him away. She had to reject him for the sake of Rhoda and her unborn baby.

"Yes, relieved, I don't care, don't love you, don't need you, you understand?"

Ben stared at her, and when he spoke, there was pain in his voice. "So you don't care, don't love me, don't need me. That's news. And here was I thinking that you did. I thought we might have a future together."

With agony, her eyes glazed with tears, she said, "With

what you have done? You have put another woman in the family way and you have the nerve to come here and tell me you love me? You are shameless! Ben, shameless! Well, let me advice you - go to the mother of your unborn baby, and make a good woman out of her."

"Whaaat?" he was stunned. Her words hit him like an unexpected punch in the gut.

He gave a cynical laugh, "This is some kind of joke, isn't it?"

"Not that I expected you to admit your shame."

"You mean you're serious about your accusation?"

"Next you'll be telling me you don't know any lady by the name Rhoda."

Ben frowned, "Rhoda? Is it Rhoda Ibitoye? What has she got to do with this?"

"For anything's sake, she's carrying your baby!" Tolu threw her hands up in the air exasperatedly.

"Whaaat? Are you accusing me of being Rhoda's lover? The father of her baby? No no no. Tell me you are joking." When there was no answer, he got up and walked towards the window, short of words. Slowly he turned back and faced her.

"I am not the father of Rhoda's unborn baby. Rhoda is Albert's woman, my cousin, if you remember him. And for the sake of the records, I don't have any lady expecting for me. I knew you, knew what you could do. I thought you knew me too, thought you would know what I could do." He shook his head in disbelief.

Tolu was looking at him in bewilderment, puzzled, as

Ben continued. "But to hear you say I put Rhoda in the family way, and worse - you believed it," he gave a dry laugh that didn't reach his eyes.

He put his hand in the pocket of his jacket and brought out a tiny jewellery case.

"It's funny how things go. I intended to give you this later on this evening. I had spent days, planning how I would propose to you, not knowing you were having your own plans as to how to shock me. You succeeded very beautifully, I must say. But my own plans are obviously no longer necessary." He threw the box on her laps.

Tolu couldn't believe what she was hearing. She was perplexed. He couldn't be saying the truth, could he? He picked the two shopping bags he brought in, and dropped them angrily beside Tolu on the chair.

"These are for you and your family and you can do whatever you like with the engagement ring in the box." With that he turned, pulled the door open and walked out, clicking the door shut behind him.

As if the sound of the car jostled her vocal cords, Tolu finally called "Ben!" she got up and ran outside. Ben had entered his car

"Ben, wait!" She walked towards his car but Ben didn't wait. He engaged the gear and drove off. Tolu walked back inside, her mouth wide open in confusion.

What had she done now? She put her head in her hands and allowed the tears to flow again, tears of despair. She had really messed up things this time.

She raised her head and picked up the bags one by one

to check the contents. There were clothes, bottles of perfume, a bag and other items she didn't bother to check, then she opened the tiny jewelry box. What she saw made her gasp! - *A diamond engagement ring.* "Oh my God!" What should she do? Could Ben ever forgive her? Sniffing, she returned the ring into the box.

She was confused. Was Ben telling her the truth? But Rhoda mentioned his name - or did she? She tried to remember their conversation that day. Then she realized that Rhoda didn't actually mention Ben, she merely said Wright. Albert too was Wright. But then, Rhoda seemed to be sure of her facts and felt she was the one after her man. If her man was Albert, how could Rhoda have come to her when she hadn't even seen Albert. She didn't know what to think. She must act fast.

She got up from the chair abruptly taking the bags with her, and walked to her room. She stopped to put the ring box in her bag and went out, locking the main door.

She took a cab to Bibi's office.

Bibi was surprised to see her, but on closer look she knew Tolu looked concerned, "What is it again, Tolu? What happened?"

"Ben came to the house this morning."

Bibi looked at her anxiously, "Did he confirm or deny it?"

Tolu breathed deeply, "It appears there is a mistake of identity."

"I knew it. What did he say?"

"I realize now that Rhoda said Wright and not actually

Ben Wright. Ben said Rhoda is Albert, his cousin's girlfriend. And his look is what is really giving me pain. He looked disappointed, and hurt, and to top it," Tolu opened her bag and brought out the ring box. She opened the box for her sister to see the ring.

"Father!" Bibi exclaimed.

"And there are two bags at home of things he got us."

Bibi looked at her with concern, "What are you going to do now?"

"I don't know, will he even want to see me again after all this?"

There was some silence. "I think you should go and see him immediately. Apologize for your rash behaviour and then discuss with him. Have a long talk."

"I'm too ashamed to go."

"Too ashamed to apologize? Tolu look, some things just have to be done. And true love is never ashamed to say sorry. If you're wrong, admit you're wrong. That's the way I see it."

Tolu raised an eyebrow. "That is If I'm wrong. How are we even sure he was not lying?"

Bibi considered what she said for some seconds. "You know him better than I do. But from the little I know of him, he couldn't have done it. But you have better judgement of him so - do you think he could have done it?"

Tolu shook her head, "No. In fact I don't know why I doubted his character at all."

"Tolu go and look for him, and have a heart to heart discussion."

"You really think so?" Tolu asked her.

"I know so. If you're getting married, you must build your marriage on trust."

"Where can I find him now? With the mood he was in when he left our house, I doubt if he would have gone back to the office, and I don't know his house."

"You don't know his house?"

Tolu shrugged, "The plan was for him to take me there today."

Bibi smiled. "That's your cup of tea. Anyway, check him in the office first. And I'd like to hear from you as soon as possible, so that my mind can be at rest."

Tolu smiled, "You have now turned to my counsellor right?"

"Yes."

****

Ben drove away in a haze from Tolu's house. A deep and overwhelming torment seemed to rage within him. He didn't know what to think again. He drove on aimlessly, torn by the conflict going on within him. He had spent the last few days thinking about the two of them being together, their marriage. He had thought they were heading somewhere, that a door was being opened for their future but now the door had slammed closed. How could Tolu do this to him? And to think she loved him!

He decided to stop at Clinton Tower for his favourite meal if that would calm his nerves. He felt unable to pray. The meal was served, and as he started to eat, he noticed some funny movement from the right side of the place. He looked up and saw a couple embracing. The blood began to pound in his heart, and feeling as if he had just been set on fire, he closed his eyes and groaned.

"Oh God what is all this?" He felt a feeling of nausea sweep over him and he pushed his plate away. He beckoned to the waiter for his bill.

He gulped down the drink he had been served and stood up. "Take, and you can keep the change."

Ben strode out and entered his car. *I'd better go home. I can't go back to office feeling this way.* Ben told himself with a hiss.

From the house, he called his secretary on his cordless phone and informed her he wasn't coming back to the office. He needed to sort some things out at home.

When he was through with her, he turned off the phone and turned it back on. Then he punched in Rhoda's office number. it beeped twice and it was picked.

"Hello, may I help you?"

"Hello, good afternoon, may I speak with Rhoda lbitoye?"

"Who is on the line?"

"Ben."

"Hello Ben - "

"Don't Ben me. Rhoda look..."

"Aah Ben, are we fighting? You've not seen me all this while and you couldn't ask of me."

"I've not seen you but I've seen your works. Do you know any one by name Tolu Pratt?"

"Yes." She said carelessly.

"Did you talk with her?"

Rhoda was getting irritated now, "Ben, what exactly are you getting at? I saw her and I gave her a piece of my mind."

Ben's face twisted in anger, "Rhoda you got the wrong person. You have messed me up. Do you know what you have done?"

"What do you mean got the wrong person?"

"Where did you see this Tolu Pratt to talk with her?"

"At Wright Investments. She's your staff."

"She's my fiancee! You wanted to quarrel with one of my staff and you didn't think you should discuss with me first!"

"I don't understand what you're trying to say Ben." Rhoda was completely confused now.

"You know the situation of things between Albert and I. He's been neglecting me because of that girl, Tolu. Have you not discussed with him a couple of times? Did he listen to you? Did he listen to even his parents? Did you think I would just fold my hands, after all I've done and suffered because of him?"

"Rhoda look, look. The other girl is Tolu Prance and not Pratt. And Pratt is the girl I want to marry. But thanks to you, she no longer wants to see me because of what you made her believe. Have I not been like a brother to you? Have I made you to lack anything you needed? I've invited you to church several times, you refused to budge. You were coming to fight a supposed rival in my office and you didn't deem it necessary to let me know..."

"But Ben, I asked of you. I was told you travelled." Rhoda said soberly.

"You could have waited!" Ben shouted. "You have messed up my life with yours now. I just thought I should thank you." Ben disconnected the call.

Rhoda was sorry. She realized her error. She couldn't afford to court Ben's anger. He had been very helpful, and even though Albert hadn't been listening to him, yet he respected Ben. Ben was a force to be reckoned with in the family, young, intelligent, rich and a Christian - he stood out.

Rhoda dialed Ben's number. It was the office she got, and Kemi told her Ben was at home. She dialed his mobile phone number.

"Ben, it's me. I'm very sorry. Is there anything I can do? Maybe to see her and explain?"

"I don't know. I can't even think straight now."

"I'll come over to her office tomorrow and apologize, is that okay?"

"Anything, what ever."

Rhoda wondered at the answers he was giving her. "Are you alright Ben?"

"Don't worry Rhoda, I'll survive,"

"Okay then, later."

Ben switched off the cell phone and tossed it aside. "Oh God! What is happening? I'm sure I prayed!"

He stopped as if to listen to God, before he continued. "Help me, I've tried, but I can't handle this. I can't force it. Have your way, Father. Let your will be done, not mine."

****

Tolu stood on the street, waiting for a cab. She hoped

she was doing the right thing. She decided to go to his office first, and if he wasn't there, the secretary might know where to reach him.

Where is a cab? - she asked with impatience, looking up and down the road. *God let a car come now* - she prayed.

Her prayer was answered as a car drew up.

"Victoria Island." She called out.

"It's 300 naira Madam."

"Okay, let me enter."She agreed, getting into the back seat of the car hurriedly. She must reach Ben by all means and immediately. She tried to ignore her fears and the nerves that clutched at her chest.

As the cab approached Victoria Island, fear suddenly seized her and she almost told the driver to take her back to where she had been picked. What was she going to tell him? She began to speak in tongues to calm herself.

The car stopped in front of Wright Ally and she stepped out. Fortunately for her, the elevator was just dropping people off. She rushed in and within seconds, she had reached his floor. She walked briskly to his office and met the secretary.

Tolu greeted her briefly, ignoring the curious look the secretary gave her as she replied the greetings. And then the most important question, "Is Mr. Wright in?"

"No, he's not."

Tolu's heart sank, but she was undeterred.

"Do you know where he might be? I need to see him immediately, it's urgent. As a matter of fact, life is involved." *Tolu's life.*

The secretary looked at her with shock displayed on

her face, and Tolu gave her a pleading look. Immediately the secretary felt concerned. Ben had looked bothered and angry earlier on, asking for Tolu, before he stormed out, and here was Tolu, also talking about "matter of life." The secretary knew something was going on, and she wished she knew what it was.

Seeing Tolu's desperation she offered. "I think he should be at home."

"Home? That's not possible. He has just ..." She trailed off. She couldn't let Kemi know he had been to her place.

"Was he not in the office in the morning?"

"He came and later went out, but he phoned to tell me he was back at home." Kemi explained.

Then curiosity getting the better of her, she commented. "I hope the problem is not so serious." She expected Tolu to fill her in, on the details of the problem.

"No no, although Mr. Wright's attention is needed. How long ago did he phone?"

"Just about twenty minutes ago."

"Hmm," that was after Ben left her house.

So he went home. Tolu wanted to be sure. "Please, could you do me a favour? Could you phone his house to confirm if he is still at home? But em - you may not mention to him that I am here. Just find something to say. You understand?" Tolu gave her another one of that her convincing innocent looks and even added a smile.

The secretary returned her smile.

"I get it." She picked her phone and dialed Ben's house. Ben picked it. "Ben on the line, who is it?"

"It's Kemi. I just want to know if you will be coming back to office today and to know how you're feeling." Kemi winked at Tolu.

"No, I don't think so." He sounded a bit odd, different.

"That's alright sir. Take care of yourself." Kemi rang off. Turning to Tolu, she said, "He's at home."

Tolu smiled at her, "Thank you. Can I have his address please?"

Kemi was surprised, "You don't have his address?"

Tolu rummaged in her bag for pen and paper. "No."

The secretary dictated the address to her. Returning the pen into her bag, she thanked her once again. "Thank you very much, I'll see you later, let me go and see him." With that she left.

CHAPTER
ELEVEN

Back on the street, she called a cab to take her to Milton Estate, Kaye street.

Before long, she was there, getting down in front of Plot 19. She paid the driver then turned to look at the house.

She was entranced by the beauty of the house that stood in front of her. It was a sprawling cream coloured two storey building.

Tolu approached the building and pressed the bell at the gate. The security man appeared and gave her a form to fill. The security man left but soon returned to open the pedestrian gate for her.

He indicated a double glass door and Tolu walked towards it. Before she could open it, the door opened from inside and a young man stood at the door smiling at her.

"Aunty Tolu, good afternoon." Tolu looked at him closely and recognition dawned on her.

"Leke! How are you? You've changed." Tolu hugged him. "It's been a long time."

"Yes." Leke replied as he led her inside the building. Straight ahead through an archway was a vast living room with chandelier and a spectacular wall of windows that looked out to the swimming pool outside.

"My brother said he's coming. You can sit down." She sat in one of the huge velvet armchairs that were scattered about the elegant room and allowed her eyes to roam around.

Leke was sitting close to the television set, with the remote control in his hand. Tolu was about to pick up a conversation with him when she had the sound of footsteps on the staircase with iron rails.

She stood up as Ben appeared, her heart beating wildly. His expression gave nothing of what he thought away and Tolu's courage almost deserted her as she watched him come nearer.

He stopped some feet away from her. He was wearing a striped shirt, pulled over a pair of jeans. Seeing him so casually dressed made her senses to stir.

"Go inside." Ben said in the direction of Leke who quickly scurried out of the room.

He moved over to the television and changed the channel, before he sat down on a three seater. Tolu couldn't help noticing that he looked tired.

She hesitated.

"Why have you come?" he asked in a low flat tone, not looking at her, as if the sight of her irritated him. She sucked in breath.

"I've come to apologize, Ben. You may not know how sorry I am." She stopped and sat down. Ben was still facing the television set.

"Rhoda came to my office on Tuesday, telling me you

put her in the family way. I didn't believe the story but her pregnancy couldn't be denied. I found it hard to believe, but she pleaded that I should give you up for the sake of her baby. My heart was breaking as I wrote the letter and even this morning, when I rejected you. I did it because of the baby."

Ben still did not say a word. Tolu got up from the chair and knelt down before him. His gaze didn't flinch from the Telly.

Tolu took his hand, "I'm very sorry Ben, can you forgive me?"

She waited.

He didn't respond.

Then he turned slowly to face her. "How could you, Tolu? How could you believe that about me? And you didn't even give me a chance to defend myself. You condemned me straightaway, calling me names. Do you think I go to church for nothing?"

"I'm truly sorry Ben, it won't ever happen again."

"Definitely. Because I'm reconsidering the whole relationship. Maybe I don't know you as much as I thought I did. Because the you, that was displayed this morning is not appealing to me."

"Ben, I've said I'm sorry. I love you."

"Love?" He said bitingly. "What do you know about love?" He hissed. "I doubt if you know what it is. I doubt if you even know what I Corinthians chapter 13 says about it." He shook his head sadly.

"Do you realize that true love always protects, it trusts, it hopes always, it perseveres. True love never fails, unlike your kind of love. I'm not sure I want any part of it." The volume of his voice was rising.

"Ben, you don't know how sorry I am."

He looked at her with regret, "Yes, I don't know, because I will never do such to you. You talked about love. Love won't criticize. I read an article that says – love will never put you down, it won't criticize you or scorn, it won't leave you forlorn. Love won't knock you to the ground. It won't verbally berate you or accuse you of not being true. Love won't increase your stress." He gave her an icy look, "Your own love has done the exact opposite. I don't want it!" He was like an angry Volcano.

Tolu flinched, "Oh my God! Ben you're hurting me," She knew she deserved his anger but she hadn't expected this much.

"You've hurt me too. Embarrassed me. Disgraced me in your family. I'm sure you mentioned it to them. Only God knows what they will be thinking of me!"

Tolu drew her lower lip between her teeth, "If it's any consolation to you, they doubted you could have done it."

Ben threw his hands up, angrily, "Great! They doubted it, but you believed it. My own woman believed I was guilty. You told me to get lost. Unbelievable!"

"Oh my God!" she repeated giving a chocked cry. She got up and sat beside him, covering her face with both hands.

Silence.

Ben looked at her. She looked so sad he pitied her. He thought of what to do.

"Look, there's so much to a relationship than physical attraction. There should be respect, trust, love that won't give up so easily."

Tolu didn't respond, her eyes were closed beneath the hands.

Ben calmed down, and took her hands from her face. "Where do we go from here?"

Tolu looked at him with sadness in her eyes. "It depends on you." She said. "Love always forgives, Ben. It doesn't insist on its own. I realize I behaved stupidly. I should have tried to hear you out, discuss with you first before taking any step."

"It's not enough. You must pay for your foolishness." He looked serious, and Tolu was half afraid of what he would say next.

"You're paying for our dinner this evening."

Tolu smiled, giving a sigh of relief. "With all pleasure."

He pulled her to him. "You got me really bothered. Only God knows what my blood pressure registered at the time l was leaving your house in the morning."

"I wasn't happy myself."

"I had planned to propose to you this evening. I'll still want to do it. Do you think you can bear to spend the rest of your life with me as my wife?"

He was holding her right hand in his own right, his left hand on her back. Tolu looked into his face with unconcealed emotions. "Oh yes, Ben, nothing will give me more pleasure."

There were questions she wanted to ask him about Rhoda.

She drew back from him. "Ben, I don't understand why Rhoda came to me, accusing me of snatching her man, do you know?"

Ben explained the telephone discussion he had with Rhoda earlier on to her. "I will want us to see her when we go out this evening. She will explain better."

"And she must apologize. I almost lost you."

Ben laughed. "I wish we could marry right away. I almost can't wait to put my ring on your finger and have you in my house . But I realize we must give time for proper courtship. How soon can we be married?"

Tolu thought for a while. "What about in four months time?"

"Four months? Can I wait that long? Why not get married as soon as possible. Do what we need to do, and forget about it?"

Tolu smiled while nodding her head. "Yeah I understand. I feel what you feel but we have to give ourselves enough time, to prepare for the wedding properly. With all the wedding plans and preparations, before we know it, the four months are completed. And in any case, don't forget you have not courted me properly. So the four months will be our time of courtship, to get to know each other better."

"It will be worth the wait." She lectured him, holding one of his hands in her two hands.

Ben pulled her to him, holding her as though he would never let go. She could feel his heart beating wildly and desire rising up in him. Then Ben lowered his lips and kissed her on the cheeks. Tolu wanted him to continue but her senses told her it would be a dangerous game. She wanted him, but it was important to her that she honoured God and be untouched by even Ben. They must not sleep together until their wedding night, that way, she would have even Ben's respect as well.

She knew she had to be strong and hold on to her sanity. She knew Ben would understand. He was matured as a Christian, even when he was not going to Church, he was the reasonable type.

She pulled away from his arms, and looked at him apologetically. "No Ben, we must wait." She said quietly. She hoped he heard her.

He did. He pulled back and dropped his hands. "I wasn't about to do anything, although I must admit I got carried away a little," he squeezed her right hand lovingly, still smiling.

"You don't know how happy I am. For the first time in a long while, I'll have a sound sleep tonight."

Ben used his right hand's index finger to tap Tolu's left cheek. "You have given me sleepless night several times, *O ti buru ju!*"

Tolu laughed at his words before saying tenderly, "I love you. I am the happiest woman on earth."

"And I thank God for making me find you again, after losing you."

"Yes. I really thank God. This God is awesome." Tolu declared in wonder. Her attention was once more drawn to the beauty of the place. She got up, walking round the livingroom in admiration with Ben's eyes trailing her.

"You've got a nice place here. I'm really proud of you. It's every bit as beautiful inside as it is outside." Her voice was enthusiastic.

"Thanks. I'm glad you love it. In four month's time, it belongs to you too."

"Nothing will give me more joy."

Ben stood up. "Let me show you round the house." He took her round and explained. To the right was the dining room, and to the left was a cozy study. Through an entrance off the living room was a large kitchen, and an area where there was a dining table and television. There was the master bedroom, guest rooms, children's rooms. Outside he showed her the swimming pool.

"Do you use it at all?" Tolu asked him.

"Sometimes. Do you swim?"

"I've never, maybe you'll teach me how."

"Willingly. I'll look forward to it." They laughed and went inside the house again.

She sat close to him, thinking of the best way to put what she had in mind. If they were getting married, they must be open and discuss freely with each other.

Courageously she started, placing her right hand on his shoulder, she picked her words. "Ben, we've known each other for long. When we used to go out together, we did everything, going all the way. We were not believers then, but now we are, and know what is right. Sex used to be an important part of our relationship, but not anymore, until we have exchanged our marital vows." She searched his face for understanding. It was not that easy for her to say no to sex too, but she knew she had to be strong for the sake of their future.

Ben looked into her eyes, grinning his familiar grin. "Of course, I know that, there's no problem, God will help us." Ben sensed passion rising within him. Just mere talking about their past sex life together was giving him the feelings. He quickly got up.

"Why don't we go out to dinner to celebrate?"

Tolu got up. "Yes. Let's go." She conceded happily.

****

"This is a fine place." Tolu commented, looking round the gaily decorated restaurant in which they were. The place was softly lit, with candles on each table. The cutleries and glasswares were of high quality. A soft music played in the background. The waiter brought the menu list to them, which Tolu handed over to Ben.

"Order for us."

Ben considered the menu. "I recommend the Oriental shrimp salad." Then turning to the man standing beside them, "Could you get us this please?"

"Hey, the ring I wanted to give you is in your house. Did you pick it at all?" Ben asked when the waiter had gone.

"Oh I've forgotten. It's here." Tolu opened her bag and brought out the small box. She handed it over to Ben.

He opened it and held the ring between his thumb and the forefinger.

"It is beautiful." Tolu exclaimed happily. It was a flawless eighteen carat diamond ring. As Ben held it up, the diamond flashed.

"I guessed at your ring size, but if it doesn't fit, it can be made larger or smaller."

Holding her gaze as if they were the only two people in the room, Ben took her left hand in his before saying, "Tolu I love you and I want to marry you." Then he slid the ring onto her finger.

****

Ben drove to Rhoda's house when they left the restaurant.

"Ben!" Rhoda exclaimed in surprise when she opened the door of her two bedroom apartment.

"How are you?"

Then her eyes flew to Tolu. "Tolu, I'm very sorry. Please forgive me for all the things I said to you that day." She threw her arms round Tolu in embrace. "Don't be offended, please."

Tolu smiled. " It's alright, don't worry."

"I was so sure…"

Ben cut in, "Aren't you going to invite us in?"

"Oh I'm sorry, do come in." She moved aside for them. "You're welcome to my humble abode."

When they entered, Ben said, "We'd like to give you the honour of being the first to congratulate us."

Rhoda looked at him, "Oh yeah? What's up?"

"We got formally engaged this evening, we'll be getting married soon," he supplied as they sat down.

"Really?" Rhoda said in astonishment. "I'm so happy for you. Congratulations." She got up slowly, a hand on her tummy, "What do I offer you? Tolu?"

Tolu raised her hand up to decline. "No, nothing for us, we've just had dinner. I asked Ben to bring me here. Why did you behave like that? You shocked me!"

"I'm sorry if I shocked you, but that should tell anyone how determined I am," Rhoda's face was serious now. "And Kunle shouldn't play games with me."

Ben shook his head in disagreement, "You didn't have to do that!"

"Why not?" Her voice was rising now. "How can he be dating another lady when I'm carrying his baby? Do you really expect me to accept it calmly? No way! I'm not a fool. He has to marry me."

"But there is a better way to handle the matter." Tolu told her in a pleading manner.

"Look, the way I see it is this, some people are so hard hearted you can't afford to play soft with them, they'll think you are a fool and take you for a ride. And at times, some don't know what's good for them until you force it down their throat."

"Not in all cases."

"I believe it will work in this my case. I believe once we're married, things will improve, he'll fall in love with me again."

Tolu was appalled. "If he doesn't love you, marriage won't make him change his mind. In fact, marriage will worsen matters because such person will be feeling tied down. He will become aggressive and resentful. It won't prevent him from having affairs. Forcing him to marry you won't solve the problem. You won't enjoy the marriage and you won't be able to come out."

"Why can't I come out? If it doesn't work, I'll know it

doesn't work, then we'll go our different ways. I'll release him."

Ben asked her, "Is that the kind of life you want? Running, all your life? Struggling? Look Rhoda, the one you need is God or else you'll keep struggling."

Rhoda sobered down and lowered her voice, "And it's been a struggle. I've been struggling to make things work for me. It's even beginning to affect my mind. It's like I'm losing my mind. Sometimes I can't sleep." She said despondently.

"And you have to get hold of yourself Rhoda, you can't afford to lose your mind." Tolu put an arm round her. "With the way you're going, you'll cause problem for yourself and you'll be endangering the life of your baby. And the love you so much desire, you won't get. Kunle won't want you under this circumstance especially if you go about threatening him and his girlfriend. You'll lose out."

"And that's what I want to prevent. I want him, I want to marry and settle down. What do I do?"

"You've got to let go and let God. Remove your hand from your life and let God put His hand. Commit it into God's hand, He knows what do, and He loves you." She looked into her eyes. "Do you know God loves you?"

Rhoda looked down, "I want Kunle's love."

"I know, that's so obvious. But you see, Ben is committing himself to me because he loves me. And because he fears God, he will be fair to me and never be unfaithful. God has to work on Kunle's life, and yours too."

Rhoda shook her head sadly, "I never planned for this that's happening to me. What have I done to deserve this,

God?" Her eyes glazed with tears.

"You haven't done anything. It's Satan that's the author of such things, but that's why Jesus came, to give you abundant life. Rhoda, trust Him."

"He impregnated me, and abandoned me," Rhoda didn't show any sign that she heard Tolu. "Is he going to abandon the baby as well, our baby? Is this how he should treat me, with all the promises he made to me?" She burst into tears.

"Rhoda pull yourself together!" Ben chided her.

"Don't cry. God will do something. He will work it out somehow."

"When will He? When?" She refused to be pacified.

God what should I do? Tolu prayed in her heart. "Crying won't solve it, neither will worry. If worry could, it would have solved it since, but I know God can. Can we pray with you?"

She nodded as she used the back of her hand to wipe her face.

Tolu prayed for her.

"Will you give your life to Jesus and accept him as your Lord and Saviour and Helper?"

"I'm ready. If that will give me peace and bring Kunle back to me."

Tolu smiled, "With God all things are possible, repeat after me, - Lord Jesus…"

When they finished praying, Rhoda apologized to Tolu again, "I'm truly very sorry for what happened the other time."

Tolu waved her off, "Don't worry. All is well that ends well."

"You're so lucky to be marrying Ben. I can see he truly loves you."

Tolu glanced at Ben, and they exchanged a smile.

"Yeah, I'm fortunate."

Ben stood up and stretched a hand to Tolu, which she took.

"We have to move. Her folks will be wondering what's happened to her."

Rhoda stood up. "Thank you so much for everything.

"We'll come and see you again, and if you like, we can come and pick you up for church,"

Rhoda smiled, "I'd love that. Thanks."

Ben and Tolu entered the car and drove towards Tolu's house.

"It's ten already. Time has gone."

Tolu smiled. "My parents will be wondering what has happened to me."

"When they see me with you, and see the ring on your finger, they will know." Tolu giggled.

****

They danced out of the church, hand in hand, looking every inch a happy couple. Tolu was radiant, looking resplendent in her wedding attire, with her face glowing as she smiled and thanked the well-wishers together with her husband, Ben.

Ben looked handsome in his well tailored black suit. During the wedding service, he had seized every available opportunity to kiss her. The Pastor had not needed to coax him into kissing the bride after the solemnization. The moment he said *you may kiss the bride* – Ben swung into action and kissed her fully on the lips which attracted cat calls, clappings and laughter from the congregation.

The choir, adorned in gold coloured robe had rendered – *Lord, you've been merciful to me* – at the request of Tolu.

Immediately after the reception, they were driven to Ben's house by his driver. They planned to go to Ben's Church the following day, which would be Sunday for thanksgiving, and then travel to London for honeymoon on Monday.

When they were finally alone, later in the evening, they sat together, talking, holding hands. Tolu looked into his face

She had thought she had lost him, but God had intervened and now he was hers.

"Do you realize if we had been married when we were still in the world, the marriage wouldn't have worked? So many things were wrong with the relationship and us, and we didn't have the *Word* to guide us."

Ben touched her face with his hand. "It wouldn't have worked. And for our sake, God separated us, got both of us converted and brought us back together again. But at the time it was happening, we must have thought God hated us, and didn't care whereas all along, He had us in mind and everything He did, was done *in love for us*.

Tolu nodded, in awe. "Hmm, you're right. Everything He did, was done... *in love for us*."

COMING OUT SOON.....

WATCH OUT FOR IT; very explosive, expressive and will leave you expressionless...

ABOUT THE AUTHOR

Taiwo Iredele Odubiyi is the associate pastor of The Fountain of Life Church Ikorodu, Lagos, Nigeria. An accountant, she holds an MBA in Finance and Management. She has a distinct and peculiar ministry to the singles and women, reaching out to them through counselling and regular hosting of the programmes *SINGLESLINK and* WOMAN TO WOMAN at the church she pastors and resides with her husband and three beautiful daughters in *Ikorodu*, a suburb of Lagos, Nigeria.

Also Coming Soon ...

...there's always light at the end of the dark tunnel !

Also on the line....

...God's love is what you need!